ACKNOWLEDGEMENTS

A number of people deserve sincere thanks for their help and guidance throughout this writing process. A special thank you goes to Karlajean Becvar. As a close and critical reader, your ideas, encouragement, and honesty were invaluable from start to finish.

I would also like to thank Jamie Bacigalupo and Belle Nelson. Your insights, as skilled readers, changed the way I viewed this story in so many positive ways. I truly appreciate your time and efforts.

A thank you also goes to my sister, Gina, who once again used her creative vision and artistic talent to capture the tone and essence of the book.

And finally, to my wife, Tara. Your never ending support inspires me each and every day. Thank you.

D1307811

THE RIDGE

Nick Hupton

NORTH STAR PRESS OF ST. CLOUD, INC.
Saint Cloud, Minnesota

Published by
North Star Press of St. Cloud, Inc.
P.O. Box 451
St. Cloud, Minnesota 56302

www.northstarpress.com   Facebook - North Star Press   Twitter - North Star Press

Prologue

ZACH DIDN'T CRY. He wanted to, but he willed his eyes to hold back the tears. His mom, however, let them go. She had been crying daily for almost a year it seemed, and today was no exception. Zach's dad even managed to shed a tear or two. This was only the second time in his life Zach had seen him cry. The other was when the policemen called Zach's house to tell his family that the search had been suspended.

The church was packed. Friends, relatives, and even some of Zach's teachers had come. He sat in the front pew next to his parents, staring at the photograph of his little brother, Chris, above the pile of flowers. Chris's pale, green eyes seemed even bigger through his thick glasses a year after his disappearance.

The pastor spoke of Chris's kind heart and intelligence. But Zach didn't listen. He just sat, staring into his brother's eyes, his mother sobbing in his ear.

PART 1

Chapter 1

ZACH KNEW WHAT HE WANTED. One more ace. Just one more and he would have a full house. "I need two," he said looking up at Logan, who was dealing the cards. Leaning over the back of the bus seat, Logan handed him two cards. Zach grabbed them from his best friend, his round, dark eyes never leaving his own set. He strategically placed the two new cards in his hand. The back of the bus was bumpy and nearly everyone had dropped his cards at least once. Everyone except Zach. He was not about to reveal his hand before it was "winning time."

Logan, Mitch, and Adam drew their cards. "Whatcha got?" Logan asked to no one in particular. Mitch and Adam glanced at Zach.

"You first," Zach said, still staring at his own cards. "But don't put 'em on the seat again. They'll slide off."

Adam flipped his long black hair out of his eyes. He showed his cards first, holding them firmly in both hands.

"Beats mine," Mitch said, his thin, Hmong eyes showing his disappointment. "Crappy pair of fours." Mitch flipped his cards, revealing the weak hand.

Zach looked up at Logan, who had slumped down a bit, his cards hidden behind the tall seat. Slowly, the cards rose above the top of the slick vinyl. Logan flipped them over slowly. Three tens.

Zach slumped back in defeat. "Crap," he said, staring at the towering, green pine trees whizzing by.

Logan grinned. They had played six games of poker on the bus ride and Zach had won every one of them.

As Logan reached down to grab his winnings of candy bars and Jolly Ranchers that had nestled up against the crease of the bus seat,

Zach grabbed his hand. "Hold on just a second," he said. "You had three tens, right?"

Logan nodded, but said nothing.

"I must have forgotten the rules for a second, because a full house beats three of a kind, doesn't it?" Zach flipped over his cards to reveal three eights and two aces. "Suckers! I'll take these, thank you very much." Zach grabbed the candy and threw it on the pile he had already accumulated in his backpack. "I believe that makes seven consecutive wins, doesn't it?"

Zach hopped off his seat, giving high-fives to two giggling girls across the aisle. He didn't stand as tall as Logan, but he wasn't short either. He had a long, narrow mouth, which allowed him his famous "Zach smile." His light freckles surrounding his rounded nose gave him a look of innocence and youth. The girls loved Zach's freckles.

Logan rolled his eyes, a slight grin on his face. "All right, I'm done," said Logan.

"But you haven't even seen my victory dance yet," Zach said, trying to stay balanced as he swayed his hips back and forth in the bus aisle.

Logan laughed.

"Zach Sutton, sit down!" Mrs. Lomeier yelled from the front of the bus.

"Whatever you say, Mrs. Lomeier!" Zach called back. When she turned her back to him, he laughed softly.

While dancing in the aisle, the jerkiness of the bus tossed him into other groups of kids, knocking his Twins baseball cap off of his head. He bent over, picked up his hat, and smoothed out the wrinkles. He felt naked without it, especially since he had lost "the bet" a week earlier.

Zach was a great baseball player. Even as an eighth grader, the Varsity coaches had scouted him on a few occasions. He was a shortstop and a pitcher. A rocket for an arm.

After practice, Zach, Logan, and three other players had been tossing the ball back and forth. Out of nowhere, Zach called out, "I bet all you fools I can throw twenty strikes in a row."

Logan and the other players looked at each other. "What are the stakes?" Logan asked.

"I'll tell you what," Zach said. "You guys don't even have to worry about it. If I don't throw twenty in a row, I'll buzz my head. If I do throw twenty in a row, we go to McDonald's after school tomorrow and you guys buy. It's a win-win for you. Deal?"

"Deal," Logan said. "I can't wait to see that bald head of yours."

Logan got behind the plate, crouched down into a catcher's position, and yelled, "All right. Throw 'em in here baldy!"

Zach stood on the pitcher's mound, staring into Logan's glove. He breathed in deeply, calming his nerves. Another deep breath. And another.

He blocked out all distractions. The other players yelling at him, the traffic on the busy street adjacent to the baseball diamond, the cool spring breeze chilling his bare arms. Nothing mattered but the leather target in front of him.

He began his windup. Strike one. Strike two . . .

Zach threw nineteen strikes in a row.

It came down to the last pitch. Another deep breath. The windup. The ball zipped through the air. Zach watched as Logan's glove moved slightly to his right. It missed the plate by about an inch. He made no argument. A bet was a bet.

Zach went to the barber the next day.

His hat now securely on his head, Zach sat, suddenly somber, staring out the window of the school bus. Minnesota's north woods flickered by. The repetition of the emerald trees mesmerized him. Shaded by the forest, Lake Superior loomed in the distance, the water stretching to the horizon.

Logan turned around to face Zach again, towering over the top of the seat. He had a long, thin face, with small, narrow eyes. Zach teased him often about his disproportionate facial features. He kept his tight, curly blond hair trimmed neatly. His sideburns were perfectly groomed into small rectangles. Zach had labeled his haircut a "halfro."

"We just passed Two Harbors, didn't we?" Logan asked. "Did you talk to your dad? Are you gonna try to see him while we're up here?"

Zach had battled his mood swings since Chris disappeared, but Logan had always seemed to be there to try to pull him out.

"We aren't going to be in Two Harbors. How would I see him?" Zach said not taking his eyes off the landscape speeding by.

Logan left him alone.

Zach had created a force field between himself and everyone else on the bus. His eyes stayed fixated on the repetition of the forest. He didn't speak for nearly an hour, not even to Logan.

Zach had been to this area of Minnesota before. His family had taken a vacation to Duluth a year and a half ago. The north woods and the ocean-sized lake were all too familiar.

Zach's brother, Chris, at eleven years old, had been two years younger than Zach. They would have been going back to school in just two weeks—Chris would be in fifth grade and Zach, seventh.

"To celebrate the end of summer," Zach's mom had said, "we're going on a fun family vacation."

But the adventure turned tragic.

Zach dodged in and out of tourists as he and his family walked around Canal Park. Little kids played in the water fountains jetting out from the brick sidewalks. Lake Superior peeked through the rows of hotels in the distance. "Come on, Chris! Let's go!" he said to his brother, beckoning him to the fountains.

"Hey, Zach, Chris. Your dad and I are going to run into that little gift shop to look for a present for your grandparents. We'll be back in five or ten minutes, okay? Don't go anywhere. Stay right here. Zach, you're in charge," his mom said.

"Okay, Mom," Zach called, still darting in and out of the water fountain.

Chris and Zach continued to run and play in the spout. Within minutes Chris began gasping for air and coughing. "Be careful of your asthma," Zach warned. "Go take a break, man."

Chris sat down on nearby steps that led to *Little Angie's Cantina*, a Mexican restaurant Zach's family had eaten at the night before.

Five minutes passed. Zach got tired of running, so he stopped. Breathing heavily, he wiped his eyes with the palm of his hand.

He looked toward the steps where Chris had been sitting. They were empty. "Chris?" he called, his eyes darting in every direction. "Chris!" he said again desperately. Zach darted up and down the sidewalk, searching every corner and every alley for his little brother. Chris was nowhere to be seen. He was gone. Missing. Vanished.

The police had searched widely, turning up nothing. No clues.

Zach stayed with his grandparents when his parents traveled back and forth from their home in Minneapolis to Duluth. They made the two and half hour trip at least once a week for a year, working with local police, and taking time off from their teaching jobs.

The only results Zach's parents had were frustration, depression, and anger. Emotions Zach sensed when his parents walked through the door after each trip.

The fighting between his mom and his dad became depressingly familiar. They fought constantly over Chris's memorial.

"It's like we're giving up!" his mom screamed.

"We aren't giving up," Zach's dad said. "I promise, I will never give up looking for Chris. I know he is out there somewhere. Just think of this as a way to pay tribute to him. It doesn't mean he's gone. I will find him. But in the meantime, let's let everyone pay their respects. It's what everyone wants."

"I don't care what everyone wants! This is our child!"

Zach heard the argument over and over. He never quite understood his dad's position. If Chris was still alive, "out there somewhere," then why bother with the memorial? His dad's famous phrase quickly became, "We'll find him. We'll find him. Don't worry." It always made Zach feel like his dad knew something he wasn't telling them. It made him curious and it enraged his mom, sparking argument after heated argument between his parents.

One year after Chris's disappearance, the memorial was held. He still hadn't been found and there still were no real clues. No one knew where he was or who had taken him, but Zach knew he was partly to blame. He was supposed to be "in charge" and he had failed. He had let Chris disappear. He had caused his parents to separate. He had made his dad move out.

Mrs. Lomeier grabbed the PA system now at the front of the bus, her caked on makeup hiding her ghostly white skin. "Ladies and gentlemen, may I have your attention please?" She waited for the thirty eighth-graders to calm down and listen. "We will be at Pine Ridge in about fifteen minutes. So, start packing up your things. When we get off the bus one of the center's leaders will be there to greet us and give us instructions. Be on your best behavior and listen carefully and respectfully." Uncharacteristically, she smiled, and said, "Oh. And don't forget, we are going to have a lot of fun up here!"

Zach snapped out of his slump and joined the other students in their cheering.

Logan got his things in order, grabbed *Eragon,* one of the three novels he was reading, opened it and tried to finish the chapter he was on before they got to Pine Ridge. "Come on, man. Can't you put that thing down for one minute?" Zach heckled, peering over the back of Logan's seat, his mood light and satirical once again.

"I just gotta finish this chapter, then I will."

"All right, nerd." Zach fell back down into his seat, then grabbed Adam and put him in a headlock for no particular reason. Just as Adam was able to free himself and have a good laugh, the bus came to a halt. A big green sign was gazing through the window at them: Pine Ridge Environmental Learning Center. Zach hopped up, grabbed his backpack, and playfully knocked Logan on top of his head, which was still buried in his book. "Let's go Einstein," he said.

"Yep, coming." Zach could hear Logan slam his book shut and stuff it in his backpack. Logan was right behind him as they headed toward the exit.

When he stepped off the bus, Zach looked around. "Dude, this is sweet," he said.

"Yeah, and just think, you almost didn't get to come," Logan replied.

"I know. My mom's freaking out right now."

Logan laughed. "You've been freaking out a little too."

"What are you talking about?" Zach asked with a smirk on his face.

"Are you serious right now? You've never got below a B until this year. And you're gettin' in trouble almost every day. I bet Lomeier has sent you out of class fifty times this month."

"You're hilarious."

"Seriously. You should be happy your mom let you come."

"She didn't just 'let me come'. I have to be a good little boy on this trip. I can't get into any trouble and I have to get all my grades up when I get back. Otherwise I have to go live with my dad in Two Harbors."

"I know, but at least you're here. Just don't screw up. Then go home and start working harder at school. You shouldn't be getting D's in eighth grade classes. They aren't hard," Logan said.

"I know they aren't hard, Einstein." Zach made his fingers into circles and put them to his eyes as if they were glasses. "Look, I don't want to move to Two Harbors. As nice as it would be to get away from *you*, it's not exactly my dream to move to Hick Town, Minnesota."

Logan laughed.

"Plus, when my parents got divorced all dad talked about was wanting to be closer to the 'scene of the crime.' He just left and took that new teaching job at UMD. I don't want to be reminded of Chris every minute of the day like he does."

"I know you don't. It's hard enough for you to deal with it now," Logan said.

"What are you talking about?" Zach asked.

"Never mind," Logan said. "Don't worry about it."

"What do you mean, 'don't worry about it?'"

"Well, it's pretty clear that you've changed a lot since Chris disappeared. No one blames you for it. I think most people would act the same way if they lost a brother like that. That's all I'm saying."

Zach turned away from Logan. He suddenly felt angry.

Logan put his hand on Zach's shoulder and decided to leave him alone. He took a step toward Adam and Mitch who were congregating nearby.

Zach stopped him. "Remember a couple of months ago when my mom threatened to make me quit baseball if I didn't get my grades up?"

Logan turned to face Zach again. "Yeah, I do."

"That never happened, did it? She never made me quit."

Logan shook his head. "Nope. And you didn't get your grades up either."

"My mom's not gonna send me to live with my dad. No way."

"Maybe not," Logan said. "But be careful anyway. Don't risk it."

Zach walked in front of Logan, leading him toward the other students. "Yeah, yeah," he said. "I'll be good, Mommy."

Logan chuckled behind him.

The teachers waited for all the students in the parking lot. Mrs. Lomeier wore a cotton-stocking cap, covering her wiry, gray hair. She directed traffic, pointing kids toward the campfire pit like an airport runway worker. Zach tried not to make eye contact with her. He was in her Science class and was getting a D. Zach was convinced she had it in for him. Sure, he would talk to his friends while she was lecturing about kingdoms or phylum, but she always seemed to pick on him when everyone else was talking too. One of the few times he paid attention in her class was when she showed a video of a previous Pine Ridge trip. It was from 1992, the first year Mrs. Lomeier had chaperoned the trip from Poplar Grove Middle School. Zach laughed at the kids' hairdos and clothes, but the trip looked awesome. He could only imagine the look on Mrs. Lomeier's pale, wizened face when he turned in his Pine Ridge permission slip.

Next to Mrs. Lomeier was Mr. Foster. Although Zach successfully avoided eye contact with Mrs. Lomeier, he quickly turned to Mr. Foster and gave him a high five. He was Zach's favorite teacher. Zach was getting a C in his social studies class, which was one of his highest grades. Mr. Foster had short, black hair and he wore jeans almost every day.

He had a lot of energy and genuinely cared about his students. Zach appreciated that.

The other four chaperones waited by the campfire pit, rounding up students. Mr. Loeb was a popular veteran English teacher, Miss Pliska, a young, pretty social studies teacher who every male student seemed to be in love with, Mrs. Connelly, a soft-spoken special education teacher, and Mr. Preston, Adam's father and the lone parent volunteer Mrs. Lomeier had conned into chaperoning the trip. Most of the students and teachers wore winter hats, gloves, and warm coats. Early April in northern Minnesota still bared harsh signs of winter.

Zach and Logan still lingered in the parking lot. The other students were running around like chickens, happy to be free of the school bus. Zach, however, stood still. An odd odor had frozen him. It made its way slowly to his nostrils. He couldn't quite put his finger on it. It was an unfamiliar smell. But it burned the inside of his nose just enough to make Zach uncomfortable.

He turned to Logan. "You smell that?" Zach asked.

"Smell what?" Logan replied.

"You seriously don't smell that? It's terrible!"

"I don't smell anything except for pine trees," Logan clarified.

"Wow, really?"

Logan just shrugged.

"That's messed up. It's burning my nose right now."

Logan looked toward the Pine Ridge campus. "Come on. Let's head over there with everyone else," Logan said, already in stride toward the campfire pit.

Zach shook his head, ridding himself of the odor. Then he tore after Logan, passing him despite his head start. When he reached the fire pit he jumped on Adam's back. "Ride 'em cowboy!" he yelled.

"Zach, please carefully dismount your horse," Mr. Loeb said.

Zach jumped off Adam's back, laughing.

The Pine Ridge campus formed a circular pattern. The buildings had an earthy, gray tone, allowing them to blend in with their surroundings.

Directly to the left of the parking lot where the students were dropped off was the rectangular administration building. Then, curving gradually up a small incline were the three dormitories the students would be staying in. Down a small hill were the classrooms, which wound around toward the campfire pit. Directly behind the fire pit was the cafeteria, hidden partially by a thicket of pine trees. Surrounding the buildings were miles and miles of forest, hills and scenery waiting to be explored.

Once all the students had made their way to the campfire pit, Mrs. Lomeier and Mr. Foster joined them. "Okay, listen up everyone," Mrs. Lomeier began. "Please get together with your roommates." The students had been allowed to choose one friend they would room with in the dorms. Four kids to a room. Zach and Logan stood next to each other. They both gazed into the crowd, looking for the other pair they would be rooming with. Michael Tynes and Tristan Phillips eased their way through the mob and stood next to Logan and Zach, refusing to make eye contact.

Zach didn't really know Michael and Tristan personally, but he had seen the bullying they suffered each and every day. He knew they were a couple of the smartest kids in the eighth grade. Right up there with Logan. But being smart wasn't the problem. Michael and Tristan were always *showing* everyone how smart they were.

At lunch one day, the two were working on math problems in the cafeteria. Zach was sitting a couple of tables away from them, talking to his friends about his three for four outing on the baseball field the day before.

His conversation was interrupted. The entire cafeteria was laughing. Michael had mashed potatoes draped all over his shirt. Someone had thrown them at him.

Zach didn't laugh.

Michael stood stiffly by the campfire pit now, watching the other groups find each other, his glasses fogging up in the cold.

Being a good three inches shorter than the other three, Tristan glanced up at Zach and Logan. When Zach turned toward him, he turned his head away and stared at the ground.

"What's up, guys?" Zach said.

"Hey," Michael said shyly.

"Hi." Tristan followed Michael's lead.

After all the groups had been assembled, Mrs. Lomeier began with her directions. "All the boys will be in cabin number one and all the girls will be in cabin number two. Your chaperones will assign you a room number when you get there. So, grab your stuff and follow either Mr. Loeb or myself."

"Let's go fellas," Zach said, picking up his bags. The four of them, along with the rest of the boys, followed Mr. Loeb to the boys' cabin. The girls walked on the other side of the path to their dorm.

Zach sprinted to the front of the line, trying to get into the cabin first. "Oh, thanks for holding the door for everyone, Zach," Mr. Loeb said as he pulled open the door and waited for Zach to hold it.

Zach put on the "Zach smile," dropped his bag, grabbed the door and said, "That's what I'm here for, Mr. Loeb. Anything I can do for you."

Mr. Loeb patted him on the head and led the rest of the group into the dorm.

After the last boy entered the cabin, Zach bent down and picked up his bag, but he paused before entering. Out past the campfire pit, where the dense pine tree line began, was a figure. Someone standing, motionless.

Zach took a couple of slow steps away from the building. He moved down the path, toward the strange sight, trying to see more clearly. But just as his eyes refocused, giving him a closer glimpse, the shadowed image turned, and oozed back into the darkness of the trees.

Chapter 2

Zach barged through the door of room number four. Logan had already claimed the bottom bunk and was lying with his head buried in his book. Michael and Tristan were playing rock, paper, scissors to see who would get the bottom bunk on their side. Logan peered over the top of his book.

"I see you took the bottom bunk," Zach said sarcastically.

"That's what you get for trying to sneak to the front of the line. You had to know Mr. Loeb wouldn't let you get away with that," he said, hiding a sly smirk behind his novel.

"Did any of you guys see something out there in the woods?" Zach asked.

Michael sat on the bottom bunk, having won the contest. He slouched forward, trying not to bump his head and rested his elbows on his knees. "What do you mean?" he asked.

Tristan climbed the ladder to the top bunk, his sleeping bag under his right arm. "What did you see?" he asked softly, tossing his tiny body and bag on to the bed.

"Let me guess," Logan chimed in. "Like the last sleepover we had, you saw the ghost of Bigfoot, followed closely by Frankenstein, carrying what must have been a corpse."

Tristan snickered from up above.

"That's hilarious," replied Zach, chucking his sleeping bag at Logan, knocking the book out of his hand. "Seriously, there was something out there, past the campfire and then it disappeared into the trees."

"It was probably just a deer," Michael said. "This area is crawling with them. Or, it could have been a wolf."

"Yeah, you're probably right. Or . . ." Zach paused for a moment. "It could have been zombies coming to eat us all!" he screamed, jumping on Logan. Logan and Zach laughed hysterically as they fell to the floor, wrestling. "Don't . . . mind . . . us!" Zach said to Michael and Tristan, gasping for air.

Tristan climbed down the ladder, laughing. Michael turned to Tristan, ignoring the wrestling match. "I think we're supposed to meet Mr. Loeb, Mr. Foster, and Mr. Preston in the lobby. Our first session is coming up soon. Come on." Leading the way, Michael walked out of the room with Tristan close behind.

"We better go too," Logan said.

"Yeah, I'll be there in a minute. You made me climb up on this stupid top bunk, so it'll take me a second to get ready. Go ahead. I'll be there in a minute."

"All right, but you better hurry or Lomeier will be pissed," Logan warned.

"Yeah, yeah. I'll be right there."

Logan left the room.

Zach sat quietly on his bed. The dense woods created a serene picture out the window. The second hand of the clock on the wall ticked rhythmically.

Zach took his eyes off the window. The odor he had smelled earlier had somehow crept into his room, finding Zach's nostrils once again. He grimaced. It was as if the smell waited until everyone else had left him alone. What is that smell? he wondered. He sat for a moment, breathing in the strange odor.

Gasoline.

Burnt rubber.

That was it. A strange mixture of gasoline and burnt rubber. It was nauseating. But as quickly as it had come, the smell disappeared.

What had caused it? And what was that figure in the woods? It was no deer, and it was no wolf. He was sure of it.

Before joining the others in the lobby, Zach rifled through his backpack, pulling out a course, glittery, white rock. His brother, Chris, had collected rocks. The day he went missing, Chris had found this one on the shore of Lake Superior. There were millions of rocks along the lake's banks. A sea of red and gray. One rock on top of another. But Chris only chose one.

One unlike all the others.

It sat on top of the pile, its gleaming white surface sparkling in the sun.

The perfect rock.

Chris had planned to add it to his collection when he got back to the hotel. He rarely left home without his rocks. Chris's collection only consisted of six stones, but they were all perfect to him. When he found one, he would tell Zach all about it, explaining its perfection. He had been really excited to add the seventh rock to his assortment. "This is the best rock of all," he told Zach.

Zach had found the stone in the hotel room before he and his parents left Duluth. No one knew Zach had kept it. Not his parents. Not even Logan. He kept it with him wherever he went.

Zach sat on the floor, the rock firmly in his left fist. He opened his hand, revealing the graininess of the gem. The rock propelled him back to the day Chris had disappeared. He gazed at the surface of the stone, remembering. Just as his thoughts drifted to a scene he had played over in his mind a million times, the fowl odor returned, pulling Zach from his reverie. Plugging his nose, he shoved the rock in his pocket and hurried out to the lobby.

When he got to the lobby, no one was there. Zach ran out the front door. Everyone was huddled around Mrs. Lomeier at the campfire pit. He slowed to a walk and strolled leisurely over to the crowd.

"Nice of you to join us, Zach," Mrs. Lomeier said. She gave him a fierce once over, the brow above her left eye touching her bangs. "I was just busy telling everyone else who made it here *on time*, that before we head off to our first class we need to assign KP duties. Kitchen Patrol. That means you get to clean dishes, set tables and serve food. All that fun stuff."

Mrs. Lomeier read off the names of the students. Each group of roommates would have KP together. Zach, Logan, Michael and Tristan were assigned Thursday during dinner. It was Wednesday, so they had a full day before they had to clean dirty dishes and slop nasty food on other students' trays.

Mr. Foster slowly made his way over and put his hand on Zach's shoulder. "Hey, Zach. Why were you late?"

"I don't know. Just had to get my things in order I guess. I took a little longer than everybody else."

"You sure everything's okay?" Mr. Foster had tried on several occasions to speak to Zach about his brother. Zach was always conscious of his mood swings in Mr. Foster's presence, knowing that he was watching him closely.

"I'm fine." Zach liked Mr. Foster. He was cool and Zach always loved social studies, but he had gotten tired of having to answer his questions. He didn't want to talk about Chris and he wished people would just leave him alone.

The students were split into two groups to attend classes. Girls and boys would be together, unlike the dorm assignments. Jenny Heeland was assigned to the same group as Zach and Logan. When her name was called, Zach nudged Logan with his elbow.

Logan grinned.

Jenny was cute. Her long, blond hair seemed to flow in the wind, even when it wasn't windy. Zach had been teasing Logan about her for weeks, ever since he had been lab-partners with her in Mrs. Lomeier's science class. She was the only person in their grade that rivaled Logan's intelligence, other than maybe Michael.

Jenny also came to Zach and Logan's first baseball game the week before. Zach was used to girls coming to his games. They came to cheer him on all the time, but when Jenny came she only watched Logan. She cheered for him when he got up to bat and even though Logan didn't get a hit that game, she came right up to him afterward and said, "You played great, Logan!" It had become one of Zach's many missions to get Jenny and his best friend "together."

Jenny's best friend, Tanya Robinson, ran over to Zach and Logan. "Hey guys! What's up?" Jenny followed behind, letting Tanya do the talking.

"What's up, Taaaaanyaaaaaa?" Zach replied playfully.

"Hey, Tanya. Hey, Jenny." Logan peered over Tanya's shoulder at Jenny's hidden face.

"Hi, Logan." Jenny slowly moved out from behind Tanya. The conversation ended there.

"All right. Let's go learn about some outdoorsy stuff, shall we?" Zach said, relieving the uncomfortable silence between Logan and Jenny.

The two groups went in opposite directions. Accompanying the fifteen students in Zach's group were Mrs. Lomeier, Mrs. Pliska, Mr. Preston, and Mr. Foster. Mrs. Lomeier led the students to a rocky path, which curved down a small hill. At the end of the path, was a short, green building with a triangular roof. A girl in a green vest met them at the entrance. As the students and teachers approached, she smiled. "Hey everyone! I'm Melanie and I'm going to be your teacher for wildlife class today." Her gold nametag confirmed her position. "Come on in."

The students and teachers filed through the door, following Melanie into one of the classrooms. Twenty chairs, facing an old, brown chalkboard, were lined up in three rows. Photographs of wolves and deer hung high on the walls.

Zach led Logan, Adam, and Mitch into the back row of chairs. Tanya and Jenny sat directly in front of them. Michael and Tristan found their way to the front row, just a few feet from the chalkboard. The teachers and Mr. Preston stood at attention in the back of the room.

Once the students were settled, Melanie began. "So, how is everyone today?"

They responded with a chorus of, "Good."

"We are so excited to have you up here at Pine Ridge. We're going to have tons of fun and learn a lot too! So, who's ready to learn about animals?"

Tristan's hand shot up in the air.

Adam and Mitch giggled at Tristan from the back of the room. Adam's dad walked up to his son and put his hand on his shoulder. The giggling stopped.

Melanie pulled out pictures of wolves, deer, and rabbits, explaining their eating habits and behaviors. She tried asking questions and engaging the students, but Michael and Tristan were the only ones participating, so she tried to speed things up. "Okay, who's ready to go outside and see if we can track down some of these animals?"

"Are we gonna get to see wolves?" Tanya asked excitedly.

"Seeing a wolf is pretty doubtful, but we may see some other cool things. Let's go out and see what we can find."

The students grabbed their jackets and followed Melanie outside. On their way out the door, Adam leaned in close to Zach. "Michael and Tristan are such dorks. It must suck rooming with them."

"Yeah, I guess," Zach said with a shrug of his shoulders.

Mrs. Lomeier surprised them from behind. "Zach and Adam! Come over here." She was serious. Adam's dad watched and listened, a concerned look on his face. "Don't you ever let me hear you talking about other students like that again. Do you understand?"

"But I didn't even say anything," Zach argued.

"Don't give me that, Zach. I heard what you guys were talking about and I don't want to ever hear it again."

"Okay, Mrs. Lomeier. Sorry," Adam said, stealing a glance at his dad.

Zach stared off into space, saying nothing.

"Zach, did you hear me?" Mrs. Lomeier asked.

"Yes. I'm sorry," Zach replied, refusing to look at his teacher.

Zach and Adam walked out the door together. Mr. Preston was already waiting outside for them. He pulled Adam aside, but Zach could still hear him scolding Adam. "We'll talk about this later," he said.

Mr. Preston walked ahead and Adam returned to Zach's side. "Sorry, man," Adam said to Zach.

"Yeah," Zach muttered.

When Zach and Adam caught up with the rest of the group, they were already in the woods, huddled on a trail surrounded by a horde of green pine trees, some of which still carried snow. Melanie was at the front of the group pointing at something on the ground. "Look everyone. Tracks."

Michael and Tristan were right up front again, bending over trying to get a closer look. "Those must be deer tracks, right?" Michael asked.

"Very good," Melanie said. "You must know your wildlife."

Michael didn't respond. He outlined the track with his finger. Tristan watched carefully.

"I want to see," Jenny said, making her way to the front of the group.

"I'll go with you," Logan said.

Zach stood in the back, still upset about Mrs. Lomeier. Adam had found his way through the group and was talking to Mitch.

"Hey, Zach." Mr. Foster's voice was unmistakable. Zach didn't look at him. "Zach, don't you want to check out the tracks?"

"No, thanks. I've seen deer tracks before."

"Yeah, but if you look real hard, maybe you'll find something else. Come on!" Mr. Foster circled around the outside of the group to get a closer look. Zach stayed toward the back by himself.

"Okay, everyone. Let's keep moving and see what else we can find," said Melanie, rising from her crouched position. But before moving ahead, she stopped in front of the entire group and spoke in a serious tone. "By the way, it probably won't ever be an issue, but be sure that you always stay with the group. Never take off on your own out here. It can be very easy to get lost in these woods. You can completely lose your sense of direction. But if you do ever get separated, my best advice is to do everything you can to find one of the trails. There are a ton of them in this area. Eighteen miles worth in fact, and just about all of them are connected in some way. So, if you stay on the paths, even though it may take a while, eventually you should be able to find your way back. But again, just stay together and you won't have to worry about it. Got it?"

A handful of students nodded.

As the pack of students followed Melanie, Michael and Tristan down the path, Logan found his way back to Zach. "What's going on?" he asked.

"Nothing."

"Yeah, right. Come on. Tell me. What did Lomeier say to you?"

"Ah, it doesn't matter, man. She's just all over my back again. Come on. Let's go up by Jenny and Tanya. Dude, she likes you. I can tell!"

By the time Zach and Logan had found their way through the crowd to Jenny and Tanya, Melanie had stopped the group again. She was pointing up at one of the tall birch trees. A spider had forged a massive web. Melanie seemed impressed, but most of the students were not. Even Michael had strayed away from the group. He was bending over, holding a jagged rock in his hands. Tristan was looking over his shoulder in admiration of the geological find. Zach watched Michael carefully as he took the rock, brushed the dirt off of it, put it up to his eyes to examine it carefully, and then jammed it into his pocket.

Zach put his own hand in his pocket. Chris's rock felt rough and cold to the touch. He gripped it tightly, assuring himself that it was still there.

Melanie guided the students through the land, curving in and out of the frost-covered woods, pointing out all the tracks, berries, nests, and animal dung she could find. The land rolled up and down, creating a seamless roller coaster. Fully recovered from Mrs. Lomeier's scolding, Zach lost himself in the terrain, sliding down slippery hills and trudging up the steep inclines, carrying his "rifle" and "taking the hill from the enemy."

Others, like Tanya, complained. "When can we go back?" she said over and over.

When the end of the class was near, the group began the trek back to the classroom. They had walked almost all the way to the other side of the camp, nearly a mile. "Wait till we get all the way to the end," Melanie yelled. "The best is yet to come!"

The students and chaperones began trudging up a small incline. Melanie stopped and pointed. "Check it out!" The hill was enormous, virtually a ninety degree cliff. Attached to it was a wooden staircase. "When you climb up the stairs, count each one. We'll see who gets the exact number when we get to the top."

"We have to climb that?" Tanya asked, exhaustion in her voice.

"Let's go!" yelled Zach, bursting through the crowd of tired campers, running into the shoulders of students.

"Zach, get back here!" Mrs. Lomeier's voice rang from the back of the troupe.

Zach stopped. He turned around, circled out from the middle of the pack, and ambled back to Mrs. Lomeier. "What did I do now?"

"Zach, you can't just run through a crowd of people like that. You have to wait your turn. You can follow everyone else up the stairs now." Mrs. Lomeier moved to Mr. Foster, who was talking with some other students. She whispered something in his ear, but Zach couldn't hear her.

Mr. Foster didn't respond.

Zach was the last one on the staircase. He casually made his way up to each landing, stopping to look out over the tops of the trees. He counted each of the steps like Melanie had told them to do. He was on 130 when he stopped at the next landing, turned, and leaned up against the railing. The higher up he got, the wider the land expanded. Lake Superior made an appearance between the trees. It was miles away. Then, through a clearing, there was a sparkle. Something metallic, maybe?

The rest of the group was almost to the top, but Zach was curious, so he sprinted back down to the bottom, skipping over stairs whenever possible. He scurried into the forest. Mud and snow splashed up on his boots as he ran. The trees hid much of the sunlight, so he stopped for a moment to let his eyes adjust. It took him a few minutes to find the glimmer he had seen before.

Finally, there it was, rammed up against a thick pine tree. As Zach got closer, he could make out its shape. An old, beat-up pick-up truck. It looked like it might have come from the 1940s or 1950s. The hood was partially open and no engine inside. Rust covered the bottom edges of the truck's frame and it sat, wedged among the trees and brush, on dirty, metal wheels.

Zach crept closer. "What a weird place for a truck," he said. Circling it, he brushed across the rough hood with his hand, picking up dust and snow. Suddenly, he realized how long he had been gone. "Lomeier's gonna kill me." But as he started to jog back to the trail, something startled him.

A tapping. Like fingernails on metal.

Zach quickly turned around.

Nothing. No sound.

"Must have been a twig snapping." He walked more slowly, waiting to hear it again.

But again, nothing.

"Yeah, just a twig," he repeated. Then he ran as fast as he could to the trail, found the staircase and sprinted to the top, counting each stair again.

Chapter 3

WHEN ZACH REACHED THE TOP of the stairs, Mr. Foster was alone, waiting for him. "Two hundred and twenty-three stairs," said Zach, trying to diffuse the trouble he was obviously in.

"Zach, where have you been?"

Zach told him the story of finding the truck.

Mr. Foster seemed disinterested. "Okay, but you can't just take off like that," said Mr. Foster. "You're in deep trouble with Mrs. Lomeier already. Do you really want to push her buttons even more? You have to stay with the group. She was ready to call your parents when you didn't come back. I had to talk her out of it. I was about to come look for you, but then I saw you running back on the trail."

"Sorry. I just really wanted to find out what it was. There's this real old truck sitting in the woods. Pretty random."

"An old truck? What are you talking about, Zach?"

"I'm serious. It's all beat up. Looks like it might be fifty years old. You might like it. You're kind of a history buff, right?"

Mr. Foster chuckled softly and gave Zach a wry smile. "Come on. Everyone else is already at the lunchroom, waiting in line. Don't do anything like that again, okay? Next time, there will be consequences."

"Can I run ahead and get in line?" Zach asked, pointing across the gravel path to the cafeteria.

"Sure, go ahead."

Zach sprinted to the cafeteria. When he reached the door, he grabbed the handle and tugged it open. But before he went in, he turned and saw Mr. Foster across the gravel path. He was looking out over the staircase, his head moving back and forth, like he was watching a tennis match. *He must be looking for the truck*, Zach thought. Then his teacher turned around, shaking his head. Zach walked into the cafeteria, disappointed that Mr. Foster had not seen the truck.

Zach was the last one in line. Both groups, all thirty students, were sitting down to eat. He saw Logan, Adam, and Mitch toward the beginning of the line, but he didn't dare budge in, not with Mrs. Lomeier watching the lunchroom like a hawk.

When he finally reached the food, students on "KP" duty dished up a bowl of soup, mushy fruit cocktail, a dry piece of wheat bread and a cookie, which was the only edible looking thing on his tray. He wished he had not hurried to lunch after all.

Zach studied the cafeteria, looking for Logan. He was sitting toward the middle of the lunchroom with Adam and Mitch. Tanya and Jenny sat at the other end of the long table, talking periodically with the boys, despite the distance between them.

Zach dropped his tray on the table, spilling the soup over the side of the bowl. He sat down directly across from Logan. "This food looks nasty," he said.

The teachers and chaperones were sitting at the next table over. Mrs. Lomeier sat down last after all the kids received their lunches.

"Where were you?" Logan asked shoveling the soup in his mouth.

"Yeah, did Lomeier get you again?" added Adam, speaking quietly so the teachers wouldn't hear him.

"When I was going up the stairs, I saw this shiny thing in the woods and I wanted to know what it was. So, I flew down the stairs and ran into the forest to figure it out. It was messed up. There was this old run-down truck in the middle of the woods."

Logan smiled. "Yeah, like there was that ghost out in the woods when we first got here, right?"

Mitch and Adam laughed.

"No, I'm serious. There's an old truck in the middle of the forest. I have no idea why it's there or what it's for. But trust me. It's there. I'll show it to you next time we're down there."

"Hey, Jenny," Zach called down the table. "If I told you there was an old, abandoned truck in the middle of the forest out there, would you believe me?"

Logan blushed. "Geez, Zach."

"What?" Jenny giggled. "What do you mean?"

"That's exactly what I mean. Would you believe that?"

"I guess I would. Why would someone make that up?"

"See?" Zach said to the others, gloating.

"Hey, look over there," Mitch said, pointing across the cafeteria. "What are they doing? I've never seen someone so infatuated with a stupid rock."

Michael and Tristan were sitting alone. The rock Michael had collected was sitting on the table in front of them. Michael examined it closely, his eyes squinting through his glasses as Tristan pointed at the different parts of the rock.

Adam laughed softly, looking over his shoulder to see that his dad and Mrs. Lomeier were still at the other table. "Seriously," he said quietly. "What dorks."

Logan picked up his tray, took it over to the trashcan, and dumped it out. Then he walked over to Michael and Tristan's table and sat down.

"What's he doing?" asked Adam.

"Going to talk to Michael and Tristan," Zach said, his hand snugly in his pocket, gripping Chris's rock. "What's it look like he's doing?" Zach got up from his seat and took his tray back to the kitchen.

When lunch was over, the students had a half hour before they had to meet for their next class. "Come on," Zach said to the others at the table. I'll take you down and show you that truck since you don't believe me."

"Are we supposed to do that?" asked Mitch.

"As long as we're back for the next class, what does it matter?" Zach replied.

Tanya overheard the conversation. "I'm not climbing up those stairs again!"

Logan was making his way back towards Zach and the others. "You in?" Zach called to him.

"For what?"

"I'm going to prove to you that the truck is really there."

"Zach, I believe you. We don't have to go all the way down there to see it."

"Oh, you believe me, now?" Zach laughed. "Let's go see it anyway. It's pretty cool."

"Fine. But we better be back in time. I don't want to miss the next class. I'm not getting reamed by Lomeier."

"Yeah, yeah. We'll be back in plenty of time."

"Let's go too," Jenny said to Tanya.

Zach smiled and gave Logan a playful elbow to the gut. "Let's go!" he said to no one in particular.

Logan, Adam, Mitch, Jenny and Tanya followed Zach out the door.

A light, April snow had begun falling on the gravel trail that connected the campus buildings. Zach started a quick jog, swatting at the flakes as they fell in front of his face. He heard the others behind him walking briskly, trying to keep up.

He passed by the campfire pit on his right and the dorms on his left, picking up the pace as he made his way down the steady, declining path.

Zach waited impatiently at the railing overlooking the stairs, jumping up and down like a runner doing a warm-up routine. When the others finally caught up to him, he said, "Who's gonna race me down the two-hundred and twenty-three stairs?"

"I'll race!" yelled Adam, running to the top of the steps.

"Let's go!" cried Zach. The two of them tore down the staircase, Zach dominating the race, as Logan, Mitch, Tanya and Jenny took their time walking behind them.

Finally, they all reached the bottom. Zach and Adam were waiting, covered in snow and dirt. "Not only did I whoop him in the race down the stairs, but he couldn't handle me in a wrestling match either," boasted Zach, gasping for breath. "Okay, you ready? Follow me." Zach veered off the trail into the woods. "It's right through these trees."

"We better hurry. It takes a while to get up those stairs," warned Logan.

"Relax, man. We'll be fine."

The kids weaved in and out of the dense forest. Zach searched for the shining light that had caught his eye the first time he saw the truck, but he wasn't able to locate it. After about ten minutes of walking through the woods, he stopped. "I think maybe we took a wrong turn somewhere," Zach confessed. "We shouldn't have had to walk this far to find it. "

"Are you seriously telling me we're lost?" Logan complained.

"Crap. My dad is going to kill me!" whined Adam.

"I swear, I went the exact same way that I did before," said Zach. "I don't understand."

"Come on. We gotta head back." Logan waved to the others and began leading them back toward the trail.

"I can't believe I have to climb up those stairs again for nothing," Tanya said.

Zach stared into the trees, motionless as the others found their way back. He turned himself around, trying to get his bearings. He was sure of it. He was sure he had led them to the right spot. It had to be. But there was no sign of the truck. No tracks. No nothing. How could that be?

The truck was gone. Vanished.

Chapter 4

W HEN ZACH RETURNED to the dorms, his group was already assembling outside the front door. He sprinted to meet them. He wasn't going to get yelled at again by Mrs. Lomeier. He knew the next time he got in trouble, his mom would hear about it and that would be a death sentence. He still wasn't convinced she would send him to Two Harbors to live with his dad, but if he was going to get into trouble with his mom, it wasn't going to be because he was late for his next environmental class. There were more interesting risks to take than that.

Zach joined the group just in time. He was able to blend in with the other students toward the back, so Mrs. Lomeier didn't notice his tardiness. Mrs. Lomeier took attendance, calling off the names of the students in alphabetical order. When she got to Zach's name, he yelled, "Here!" from the rear of the group.

Logan was standing near the front with Michael and Tristan. He turned around at the sound of Zach's voice and gave him an approving smile.

Before they had left for Pine Ridge, Zach had told Logan about his mom's threat to send him to live with his dad.

When Logan had heard the news, he let Zach have it. "You can't move! With my luck, I'd end up getting some old farts for neighbors. Plus, who are you going to beat up on in HORSE? You have to stay. So, here's the plan. You will not screw this up. You're going to get your grades up and you won't get into any more trouble."

Logan had sounded like Zach's mom, always nagging him. But he was also flattered by his best friend's concern. Zach understood Logan's point of view. He didn't want to leave his best friend either.

Mrs. Lomeier continued taking roll. Logan's curly hair popped up above the other students. His hair was longer now than the first time Zach had seen the "halfro". They were only eight years old that day when Logan moved next door to Zach.

"Hey! Curly hair!" Zach called. "Want to come over and shoot some hoops? Me and my brother are playing HORSE."

Logan sat on his back steps, his head resting on his hands. "Me?"

"Yeah, come on over. You don't want to help your mom and dad move stuff, do you?"

"No, I guess not," Logan said, slowly walking down the steps.

Zach tossed him the ball. "Let's see your jump shot," he said.

Logan tossed the ball at the hoop and it clanged off the rim.

"Try it again," Zach said.

This time Logan stepped closer and tossed the layup through the net.

"Not bad," said Zach. "Come on, let's play a game."

They played five games of HORSE and as they shot, Zach bombarded Logan with questions. "Where are you from?"

"Rochester. My mom and dad are artists."

"What kind of art? Like painting?"

"Yeah, I guess. They draw stuff too."

"How come you moved? What's wrong with Rockaster?"

"Rochester. They moved for their jobs, I guess."

"You have any brothers or sisters? This is Chris. He's my younger brother."

"You already told me that. I don't have any brothers or sisters."

"What about sports? You play any sports? Looks like you're okay at basketball."

"I play baseball, too."

Zach smiled. "Me too," he said as he drained the winning shot. "You should sign up for my team. We won our league last year."

Logan nodded.

Zach won all five games of HORSE. "This is the worst I've ever been beaten," Logan claimed.

Zach tried to help Logan out by lowering the hoop to nine feet, but still, Logan couldn't keep up with him on the court. "You wanna do something else?" Zach asked.

"I should probably go back and help my mom and dad, but can I come over and play again? We don't have a hoop in our backyard."

"Yeah. Come over whenever. You could use the practice," Zach said with a smirk.

Logan looked back at Zach as he made his way to his house and smiled.

"It looks like everyone is here." Mrs. Lomeier's voice startled Zach.

The students were buzzing. They had just been told about their next class. They were going to be working on "team building" and "facing fears" while trying to conquer Pine Ridge's ropes course.

Zach and his classmates walked down the gravel path, but this time they veered off to the right, past the triangular classroom building, and headed down an even steeper hill.

In the distance was the ropes course, its towering structure looming through the green pine trees. When the students and chaperones reached the course, a new instructor awaited them. "Hey everyone! I'm Manny. Welcome to the ropes course." Manny was roughly six feet tall, with jet-black hair and sandy brown skin. He wore the same green employee vest with his nametag on it, just as Melanie had. "This is the moment you've all been waiting for, right?" he asked.

A chorus of, "Yeah" resonated throughout the group. Mr. Foster, Mrs. Lomeier, Mr. Preston, and Mrs. Pliska shared smiles with each other.

Pine Ridge's ropes course was legendary. It was one of the reasons the trip was so popular. In Science, Mrs. Lomeier showed a video of students on the course. Zach had looked forward to the challenge ever since.

Manny continued. "You see that big, daunting apparatus over there?" He pointed up to the ropes course.

The students nodded.

Zach smiled as Jenny and Tanya looked on with horror.

Manny moved closer to the students, looking them all in their eyes one at a time. "In a couple of hours, I'm confident that all of you will have conquered it in your own way. For some of you it might mean that you simply get up there and give it a try. Even if you don't finish the course, trying something scary is an accomplishment. For others, you might run through this thing three or four times, but remember, it can be different for everyone. And that's okay."

"We can go on this thing more than once?" Zach blurted.

"Some of you might. If you're up for it, there should be time," Manny said. "But before anyone conquers this thing, we need to have a little training session. Follow me," he said with a wave of his hand.

The students followed Manny up five stairs to an open-air shack. There were cabinets filled with harnesses and karabiners. Manny took one of the harnesses out and began demonstrating the proper usage of the device. Then he began handing out the other harnesses to the students, checking the sizes of each.

"Okay," he continued. "All of you need to grab a partner."

"What do we need partners for?" Zach asked.

"Your partners will double check that the harness is on correctly and he or she will be each other's motivators on the course. You need to offer encouragement to each other. For a lot of you, this is going to be a bit scary, so your partner will help you through it."

The students partnered up by standing next to each other, the teachers intervening when necessary. Zach stood with Logan. Tanya with Jenny. Adam with Mitch. And Michael with Tristan.

Tristan looked nervous. He stared at the intimidating course with his mouth slightly open.

"Are we all set?" asked Manny. "Then let's go!" Manny led the students down to the entrance of the course. "When you enter the course, you must first clip your karabiner to the attachment." Manny demonstrated and then climbed up to the first obstacle, a single walking rope with two parallel ropes to be used as railings. It was suspended fifteen feet above the ground. Manny began balancing his way across the rope, holding on with both hands. Suddenly, his feet slipped out from under him and he slid off.

The students gasped.

Zach laughed along with Manny as he hung from the structure by his harness. "See, even if you fall, as long as you have your harness attached, you can just hang here. It's actually kind of fun." Manny swung back and forth, kicking his legs out like a child. Then he regained his balance and continued through the course, demonstrating each obstacle along the way.

The second obstacle was a sloped wooden bridge that inclined toward the middle tower on the course. Manny clipped his karabiners to the wires directly above him, reached his arms up, grabbed the straps and sprinted up the bridge, landing on the tower's platform. "That one's a piece of cake!" he called down to the students below.

The third obstacle took a sharp, ninety-degree turn. Manny unclipped his karabiners, one at a time, and reattached them, one at a time, to the post on the new obstacle. "Did everyone see what I just did? This is one of the most important rules. Your partners and the chaperones who will be up here on these platforms will help to remind you, but you must always be sure that one karabiner is attached to the course at all times. Never take both off at the same time. Everyone understand?"

The students nodded.

Zach could see Tristan out of the corner of his eye. He stared, wide-eyed, at the structure.

Manny climbed on to the third obstacle: two thick, wooden logs. Again, he held the two straps above his shoulders for balance, the karabiners firmly attached. Then he smoothly walked over the two logs.

Reaching the third tower, Manny unhooked one karabiner at a time and then demonstrated obstacle number four. This challenge was similar to the first. It required a balancing act on a thin tightrope-like cable. Only this time, there were no hand cables to hold on to. The two harness straps were clipped to a cable above. Manny held the two straps for balance.

Zach ran to the front of the crowd to watch Manny scale the difficult task, passing Tristan who had since left the group to sit on a nearby bench. "When you reach the final tower, the best is yet to come!" Manny called as he wobbled his way across the tightrope. Climbing up on the final tower, Manny, once again, unclipped each karabiner separately, and then reattached each to the final, culminating event. "This is what you've all been waiting for . . . the zip line!"

"Yeah!" screamed Zach. The other students quickly followed Zach's lead by cheering and hollering. Manny clipped his harness to the thick, sturdy cable, sat back, lifted his feet up, and took off down the line, spinning and laughing as he went.

Zach sprinted after Manny, hoping to see the conclusion of the ride. Adam and Mitch followed closely behind. "That was awesome!" Zach said as Manny climbed out of his harness. "Me and Logan want to go first."

Manny chuckled. "Okay, okay. Let's go get everyone situated and we'll see. Everyone will get at least a couple of turns on this thing."

The chaperones went up first, so that they could "man" the towers. Mr. Foster would be on the final zip line tower, Mrs. Pliska on the third tower, Mr. Preston on the second, and Manny would handle the first tower. Mrs. Lomeier would stay on the ground to keep order.

Zach and Logan had managed to budge to the front of the line, so they would be the first students up on the course. One student would make their way through the course, while his or her partner would be the "motivator" as Manny put it. In Logan's case, he would stay on the ground, tracking Zach and cheering him on. "Your job is going to be pretty easy!" Zach called. He knew he wouldn't need a lot of help.

Zach eased his way through the obstacles with little trouble. At times, he would purposely fall off the course as Manny did, causing Mrs. Lomeier and Mrs. Pliska to gasp. When Zach reached the final tower, Mr. Foster congratulated him, unhooked his karabiner as Manny instructed, and locked him on to the zip line.

"See you later, Zach!" yelled Mr. Foster as he pushed him off the tower. Zach went cruising down the line, relishing the brisk wind whipping against his face. Logan smiled and ran to meet Zach at the end of the zip line, giving him a high five.

Zach was the ultimate "motivator" for Logan, who was a bit more timid on the course, but still made it through with very few glitches. He encouraged him at every stop and at anytime Logan felt nervous. Zach knew when Logan needed help. That was part of being his best friend.

There had been an unspoken vow between Zach and Logan. When Zach's brother went missing, Logan was there for him. The sleepovers. The days after school at Logan's house when Zach just didn't want to go home. The science fair Logan skipped earlier that year because Zach's dad had just moved and Zach didn't want to be alone with his mom. Logan had always been there for him and Zach pledged to do the same for Logan.

It took nearly an hour for the students to go through the course once. Zach scanned the grounds for anyone who hadn't gone yet. Tristan was still sitting on the bench. "Hey, Tristan!" he called. "Are you going to go up on the course?"

Tristan shook his head, his eyes staring at the ground. Zach paused momentarily, immediately sorry that he called Tristan out so publicly. Then he turned around and called to Manny. "Can we go for a second turn now?"

"Yeah, I think so."

"Nice." Zach turned to Logan. "Watch what I can do on this run."

"Zach, what are you gonna do? Don't do anything stupid."

"Trust me."

Zach climbed up to the first obstacle. "Okay, clip your karabiners to the cable," yelled Manny.

"Don't worry. I got this." Like a circus performer, Zach proceeded to climb out on the shaky, single cable without attaching his harness to the structure. He was walking with no support. Zach proceeded to climb out on the shaky, single cable without attaching his harness to the structure.

"You have to attach your harness. Don't come any farther!" Manny screamed.

"Zach, what are you doing?" questioned Logan.

"Don't worry. I'm fine!" Zach replied, holding his balance and looking down at his feet as they pushed across the cable.

Mrs. Lomeier came scurrying over, positioning herself directly below Zach. Manny continued to yell to Zach to attach his harness.

"Zach, go back the way you came. Right now!" Mrs. Lomeier yelled.

Zach ignored the pleas and continued to make his way across the tightrope. With little difficulty, he made his way to Manny's tower. Manny grabbed him and pulled him on to the platform. "What's your name?" Manny asked sternly.

"Zach Sutton," he said proudly.

"Zach, what you did just now was very stupid and you could have been seriously hurt or even worse. We don't tolerate that kind of behavior out here. I'm going to attach your karabiners and you need to go back over that cable, take off your harness, and then you are done with this ropes course. Do you understand?"

"Yeah, I understand."

When Zach got down from the structure, Mrs. Lomeier was waiting for him. Zach saw Logan watching out of the corner of his eye. He looked worried.

"Zach," Mrs. Lomeier began. "In my twenty-five years of chaperoning this trip, I have seen some really stupid things. This is by far the dumbest. It's one thing to be goofing around in class and to blow off your homework, but you just put your life in danger. I don't understand what you were thinking. We'll need to deal with this later, but for right now, you need to go sit on that bench and I don't want you to move the rest of the evening."

Zach walked over to the bench, passing Logan. "You know what this means, right?" Logan whispered to him as he moved toward the bench.

"Maybe. We'll see," said Zach.

Zach sat down at the end of the bench. His mind raced. *I am so sick of Lomeier being all over my back,* he thought. Because of her, my life is over now. Two Harbors, here I come. I could have finished that whole course on my own. No harness. Even if it *was* dangerous, what did it matter anyway? I could die tomorrow, or just disappear. I might as well enjoy life while I have the chance.

Zach took off his Twins hat and rubbed his cold hand across the top of his buzzed head. He wished he had brought his warm winter hat. Then reaching into his pocket, he gripped the grainy, rough rock and remembered Chris. He wished the rock would transport him back in time, to a place where Chris still laughed and played. His mom would be there. Chris and Zach would be there. And his dad would be there. Not in Two Harbors.

Tristan was still sitting at the edge of the bench. Zach slid down to Tristan's side, leaned back and folded his arms behind his head.

Tristan turned his head away.

"Tristan," Zach called. "How come you aren't trying the ropes course? It's pretty sweet."

"I just don't feel like it."

"Are you scared of heights or something? It's not a big deal. That harness catches you even if you do fall off."

"Not if you don't attach the harness," replied Tristan.

"Good point. Good point," said Zach with a smile, appreciating the subtle shot Tristan had just taken at him. "You know, my brother was afraid of heights. My mom took us downtown this one time. We went to the top of the IDS building. Chris wanted nothing to do with it. He stood by the elevator the entire time. He wouldn't come close to the window. Of course, he was only eight years old at the time, but still, I get it."

"I just don't want to go up there. That's all," Tristan explained.

"All right, all right. I get it. But . . . what if I was your trusty 'motivator?' I could help you get through it. Michael's over there about to get on the zip line again. Whadda you say?"

Tristan was silent.

"Come on. Let's go." Zach looked around for Mrs. Lomeier. She had moved toward the middle of the course, her back turned to him and Tristan. Zach grabbed Tristan's arm and pulled him off the bench.

"Zach, I don't want to do this!" Tristan called.

Zach pulled him over to the start of the course, grabbed an unused harness, and helped him strap it on. Tristan's eyes were wide and full of fear.

Manny was watching the two, but Zach continued anyway.

Once the harness was securely on, Zach nudged Tristan up to the first obstacle. He gingerly climbed the ladder to the entrance platform, looking back to Zach for assurance. "You got this, man," said Zach.

"Okay, buddy," Manny called from the second platform. "You can do this!" Manny then walked through the instructions for connecting Tristan's karabiners.

"Take a big, deep breath before you start," Zach said from the ground below. After a long pause, Tristan finally took his first step on to the shaky cable. "There you go. Just like that. Good. Now take another step." Zach talked Tristan through the first obstacle. Manny stayed quiet, not interfering with Tristan's progress.

When Tristan reached the platform, he sighed with relief.

"Nice work, Tristan!" called Zach.

"Thanks, Zach," he yelled down.

"Okay, let's move on to the next one," Zach said.

"Zach Sutton! Sit back down on that bench. You are not supposed to be up," yelled Mrs. Lomeier, striding toward him.

"I was just helping Tristan through the course." Zach thought the excuse was legitimate.

Mrs. Lomeier looked up to Manny.

Manny nodded.

"It doesn't matter. You are not supposed to be participating anymore. Sit back down on that bench until we are finished."

Tristan looked lost as Zach slid over to the bench. As he sat down, Tristan was about to take his first step on to the wooden bridge. Zach gave him a "thumbs up" and Tristan took a step.

A half hour passed before everyone was finished with the ropes course. The students filed out of the area, thanking Manny.

"Hey, Zach," Manny called as he organized the harnesses in the storage cabinet. Zach pulled out of the group and walked over to Manny in the storage shack. "I wanted to let you know that the stunt you pulled out there was not very smart. You really took a huge gamble. Next time, think before you act, okay?"

"Yeah, okay," Zach said.

"But I also wanted to say thank you. Tristan never would have conquered his fear if it wasn't for you."

Zach nodded and turned around to catch up with the group. *Where was I when my brother needed help?* he thought.

The pack was far up the trail. Zach was tired and didn't feel like running to catch up with them. He was alone.

A strange knocking came from the woods, like a hammer on a tree. Zach stopped. Turning toward the sound, he stepped off the trail, into the trees.

Knock . . . Knock. The sound was louder now. Zach's shoes were buried in the dirt and snow. He was scared to move. Then the knocking stopped momentarily, so he pulled his feet from the ground and took another step deeper into the woods.

In the distance, behind a thick pine tree, a faint glow illuminated the surrounding forest. Then the familiar odor oozed through the trees to Zach's nose. He took two more tentative steps toward the light and then . . . darkness.

No knocking. No glow. No stench of burning rubber or gasoline.

A shiver traveled up Zach's spine. What was out there? Was something following him? He didn't want to find out.

He turned and sprinted back to the trail, hoping to catch up with the rest of the group. After all, there was safety in numbers.

Chapter 5

It was dinnertime. Zach was the last person to reach the dining hall . . . again. When he got there, Mrs. Lomeier was waiting for him. "Where have you been?" she asked with her piercing snake eyes.

"Mrs. Lomeier, you won't believe what I just saw out in the woods. Did you see that glowing thing out there?" Zach gasped for breath. Despite being in excellent shape, the brisk air had made it difficult to run.

"Zach, I don't want to hear it. Come with me."

"But I swear, there's something out there!"

Mrs. Lomeier ignored him.

Zach followed her as they walked toward the administration building. "Where are we going?" he asked.

"We're going to call your mother and tell her about the stunt you pulled on the ropes course."

Zach's gait slowed. "You can't call my mom! She'll kill me! She'll probably send me away to live with my dad."

Mrs. Lomeier turned around to face Zach. She paused, looked at the ground, and then looked at Zach again. Quietly, she replied, "You should have thought about that before you put your life at risk. I'm in charge of all of you. I have a responsibility to inform your mother about that kind of behavior."

She turned and opened the door to the admin building, waving to Zach to follow her in.

Zach stood his ground, and then spoke softly to himself. "It's my life. Why can't I risk it? We don't control any of it anyway."

He took a deep breath and clasped his fingers together on top of his baseball hat, helping him warm his chilled, buzzed head. Then he followed Mrs. Lomeier into the building.

When he entered, Mrs. Lomeier was standing in the lobby, her cell phone in her hand. The only other person in the room was the secretary at the information desk. The desks behind her were empty and the lights dim. The secretary's eyes looked pitifully on Zach.

"Will you give me your phone number please?" Mrs. Lomeier asked.

Zach was a bit surprised. He was sure she would have had it memorized by now. Mrs. Lomeier had made numerous calls to Zach's mom to discuss his "inappropriate behavior" and his "poor academic effort." "952-555-9962," he said.

Mrs. Lomeier dialed the number. It seemed to take an hour to place the call. He grimaced with the "beep" of each button. He could hear the faint ringing from where he stood.

"Mrs. Sutton? This is Patricia Lomeier, Zach's Science teacher. Yes. I'm calling from Pine Ridge and I wanted to talk to you about Zach's behavior . . ."

A small sofa sat near the entrance of the lobby. Zach sat down on it. He listened to Mrs. Lomeier tell his mom about his antics at the rope course.

He was tired of getting into trouble. He was tired of teachers calling his mom. There was a time when things were different. A time before his grades and behavior had slipped, and a time before Chris had disappeared.

Report cards had come out. Zach was in sixth grade. He had received all A's and B's. Chris was in fourth grade. His report card had all A's. Zach's parents were proud. They would all go out to celebrate at Red Lobster. He and Chris loved the popcorn chicken. As far as Zach was concerned, there was nothing better.

The two boys sat on one side of the booth, their parents on the other. After ordering their food, they held a tic-tac-toe tournament on their napkins—a Sutton family tradition. Chris played against his dad and Zach against his mom. The semifinal matches were a foregone conclusion. Zach and Chris always played in the championship.

Zach went first, strategically placing an X in the center spot. Chris countered with on O directly below the X. The battle seemed endless, carrying on for a good three minutes.

In the end, Zach had won, but Chris had made it clear that if he had gone first and placed his letter in the middle, he would have won.

Zach considered it a mere technicality. But he also knew Chris was right. There was no skill involved in tic-tac-toe.

When the food came, Zach and Chris devoured it, while their parents explained to them the schedule for the week. "On Saturday, Zach has baseball practice and Chris has the science fair, so we'll have to figure out how to juggle that," their mom said.

"I can bring Zach to practice and afterwards we can come right over to Chris's fair," said Zach's dad.

"You're in that science fair again?" Zach asked Chris.

"Yeah, I made a little machine that automatically waters your house plants. It works on a timer. Mr. Jensen helped me with it quite a bit."

"Do I have to go again this year?" Zach asked his parents. "I can see Chris's invention when he brings it home. I don't need to go. Those things are always so boring."

"Chris comes to all your baseball and basketball games. You will go to his science fair," said Zach's dad.

Pouting, Zach put his head down and doodled on his napkin. Chris gave no response to Zach's protest. He simply grabbed a blue crayon and colored in the fish on his kids' menu.

Zach followed his family out of the restaurant. His mom and dad held hands through the parking lot and Chris, a few paces ahead of him, jumped over each painted parking space line.

Zach was quiet the whole ride home. He stared out the window and thought about all the baseball games Chris had come to. All the times he had cheered him on from the bleachers. Chris *had* always supported him.

Zach never apologized to Chris for that night.

"Zach . . . Zach?" Mrs. Lomeier held out her phone. "Your mom would like to talk to you."

Zach stood up, bracing himself. He took the phone from Mrs. Lomeier. "Hello?"

"What were you thinking? You could have been killed!" His mom was irate. "I am tired of getting these phone calls from your teachers, Zach. Don't you remember the conversation we had before you went on this trip? Didn't it mean anything to you?"

"I remember, Mom."

"So what am I supposed to do about this?"

"I don't know."

"That's all you have to say? You don't know? Maybe we need to re-visit it then. Maybe you *want* to go live with your dad."

"Mom, do we have to do this right now?"

"We'll discuss this further when you get home. Don't get in any more trouble before then, you understand?"

"Yes, I understand." Zach handed the phone back to Mrs. Lomeier. "Can I go eat now?" he asked.

"I'll walk you over there." Mrs. Lomeier said goodbye to Zach's mom, hung up the phone, and thanked the secretary.

ZACH WENT THROUGH THE dinner line, remembering that the next night he would be on Kitchen Patrol. He was the last one to get his food, but luckily there was still enough left for him. Logan was sitting with Jenny and Tanya. Adam and Mitch had already finished eating and had gone outside. He sat down next to Logan.

"Where have you been?" asked Logan.

Zach explained how Mrs. Lomeier had called his mom.

"Geez, Zach. Well, you can't be surprised, right? That was a pretty crazy thing you did out there, even for you."

"I s'pose."

"What's your mom gonna do?" asked Tanya.

"I don't know. We're gonna talk about it when I get back. It's not going to be good though."

"Two Harbors?" asked Logan nervously.

Jenny and Tanya looked confused. Zach had only told Logan about his mom's ultimatum. "Don't know." Zach quickly changed the subject. "Hey, did any of you see some weird glow in the woods after the ropes course?" he asked.

Logan laughed. "You're still trying to scare us with that crap?"

"No, I'm serious. Something was out there. It made this creepy knocking sound too."

"I think you're seeing things," said Logan.

An old woman, dressed in a pure white uniform, wearing a hairnet, was wiping down one of the empty tables across the room. Zach had seen her working in the kitchen at other mealtimes. She looked like she had been around Pine Ridge for a while. He wanted answers and he was getting no help from his friends. So, he finished his dinner, put his tray away, and approached the woman.

Zach stood behind her and tapped her on the shoulder.

Startled, she spun her ahead around and dropped her washrag. She had wizened, droopy skin, and a short stocky build.

"Hi . . . Miranda," Zach said, looking at her nametag.

"Hi. Can I help you?"

"Yeah. Question for ya."

"Okay. I'll see if I can give you an answer." Her voice was scratchy, as if it had spoken to thousands of kids like Zach over the years.

"Do you know anything about an old pickup truck in the woods? I saw one near the huge staircase, but when I went back to find it again, it was gone."

Miranda bit her bottom lip and her eyes opened round like a cat's. "You saw a pickup truck in the woods?"

"Yeah, I did, but I have no idea what happened to it. It's like it just disappeared."

"Uhh . . . well, no. I don't know anything about a truck. That seems odd." Miranda fumbled with her speech. She seemed to be searching for an answer.

"Really? You've never seen one down in the woods? How about a strange glow in the forest? Ever see anything like that?" Zach decided to press further.

"Uh, son. I'm real sorry, but I have to go finish cleaning the kitchen. Lots of work to do. And I think you need to get to that campfire. Your classmates are already out there. Sorry I couldn't help you more." Miranda waddled quickly toward the kitchen. When she reached the kitchen door she paused, turned around, and looked at Zach with the paleness of someone who had just seen a ghost.

Chapter 6

ALL THIRTY STUDENTS AND chaperones huddled around the bonfire, roasting marshmallows and making s'mores. The teachers and Pine Ridge employees took turns entertaining the kids. Mr. Foster and Ms. Pliska sang a duet of Vanilla Ice's "Ice, Ice Baby." It was purely coincidence that both knew the entire song and the dance moves that went with it. "There was no rehearsal here," Mr. Foster bragged. The group of eighth graders laughed hysterically. All of them except Zach. He isolated himself, sitting alone on one of the wooden benches, not wanting to take part.

Mr. Foster gradually made his way through the crowd toward him. Zach knew what was coming. "Hey, Zach. What's up?" he said, sitting next to him on the bench.

"Nothing, Mr. Foster." He just wanted to be left alone.

"I heard that Lomeier called your mom. You know, she didn't have much choice. That was a real dangerous thing you did out there."

"I know."

"Well, if it means anything to you, I am proud of how you helped Tristan. I bet he'll remember that for a very long time."

"Yeah, we'll see. Maybe he won't remember it at all. Maybe everything we do right now is pointless. Because it's all going to end anyway."

Mr. Foster's upbeat, positive demeanor disappeared. He put his hand on Zach's right shoulder. Zach still stared straight ahead. "Why do you say that?" he asked.

Zach shrugged his shoulders.

Mr. Foster sat with Zach for a few more minutes. "You want to come up and join the group?" he asked. "Maybe have a s'more or something?"

"No, thanks."

"Okay. Well, you hang in there. And remember, if you ever need someone to talk to, you know where to find me. Okay?"

Zach nodded.

Mr. Foster stood up and walked back to the rowdy group of students.

Logan and Jenny were busy roasting marshmallows around the fire. They laughed as they tried to dodge the smoke that attacked them from all angles.

Logan stopped laughing. The glow of the fire illuminated his face. He looked through the crowd at Zach, whispered something to Jenny and then made his way over to him. Sitting next to him on the wooden bench, he asked, "You all right?"

"I'm fine. I just don't know what my mom is gonna do when I get home. But honestly, I'm not sure if I care anymore either."

"What do you mean? You want to go live with your dad?"

"Well, I don't want to move away from you guys, that I know. But the more I think about it, the more I understand why my dad moved. To escape everything. I kind of get it."

Logan nodded, listening.

"I don't know. We'll see what happens, I guess," Zach said. He quickly changed the subject. "You don't believe me about the stuff I saw in the woods, do you?"

"I don't know. Maybe you saw something, but it could be anything."

"What about the truck? What about the figure I saw when we first got here? They can't all be figments of my imagination."

"You're pretty stressed out. Maybe that's part of it."

Zach just shook his head. "So, you and Jenny are moving along nicely, huh?" he said, nudging Logan in the gut with his elbow.

"I like her. She's cool."

"She's a little more than cool, don't you think?" Zach said, grinning. "You shouldn't be back here hanging out with me when your girlfriend is up there roasting marshmallows for you. Get outta here!"

"She isn't my girlfriend." Logan smiled. "But okay, I'll go back. I could use another s'more."

Zach grinned as Logan made his way through the crowd, searching for Jenny. He found her close to the fire talking to Tanya, Adam and Mitch.

Zach watched as his best friend captured the attention of one of the cutest girls in the eighth grade. He watched proudly, feeling somewhat responsible for the connection the two had made.

But his brief happiness quickly vanished.

A light touch tickled the back of his neck. He turned around to see the culprit, but nothing was there. Only darkness. It must have been the wind.

He got up, ready to make his way to the fire to join the festivities. But before he could take a step, the hairs on the back of his neck stood up. Zach spun all the way around, searching for the source, but again, nothing.

He glanced at the leaves on the trees. They were as still as a calm lake at dusk. No wind. He stepped away from the benches surrounding the campfire circle. He crept toward the dormitories across the gravel path, searching for answers. Other than the lights lining the path, there was only darkness.

Zach put his right hand in his coat pocket and clutched Chris's stone. He turned back toward the campfire.

Waiting for him at the edge of the campfire circle was Miranda. She was dressed in her civilian clothes instead of her white kitchen uniform. Her face was dark, hidden by the blackness of the night. "You never told me your name," she said.

"It's . . . Zach," he said nervously.

"So, Zach . . . You say you saw an old truck in the woods?"

Zach was suddenly interested. "Yeah, I did. Do you know something about it?"

Miranda stared deeply into Zach's eyes. "I think it's time for ghost stories around the fire," she said. "The Pine Ridge teachers always tell some good ones, but I have a story you may be more interested in. Come with me." She grabbed Zach's hand, looked around carefully, making sure no one had seen them, and then led him across the gravel path to a bench, partially hidden by trees.

Zach sat at the edge of the bench, the glow of the campfire in the distance. He waited impatiently for Miranda to begin.

Miranda inched toward the middle of the seat. She stuck her short, wide neck out as far as she could, trying to get Zach's attention. Then she began. "For a long time, rumors have circulated throughout Pine Ridge of a haunting."

Zach scooted up to the edge of his seat. He gazed into her solemn eyes.

"I have been working at Pine Ridge ever since it opened. Close to thirty years now. The stories have flown around here in different forms for as long as I can remember, but to most people, that's all they are— stories. Until tonight. You're the first person I've met who has seen the truth."

"What is the truth? What's out there?" Zach asked.

"Son, I'll get there. Don't you worry." Miranda breathed in the fresh, cool air and patted Zach on the knee. She continued. "Well over one-hundred years ago, long before Pine Ridge existed, this area was settled and the main industry was logging. As more people came to take advantage of the trees, the town of Finland was created, which is right down the road from here. The town did pretty well.

"In the 1920s, two of the more powerful families in Finland were the Sutinens and the Lepplas. Both families owned their own logging businesses and became peaceful rivals because of that." Miranda scooted closer to Zach. "But the peace didn't last."

Zach's eyes widened.

"Fredrik Sutinen, who was the head of the Sutinen logging 'empire', was elected mayor of Finland. People really liked him. He was like royalty around these parts. Plus, many of the townspeople worked for him, which took workers away from the Leppla business. The Sutinen Company thrived. This made Victor Leppla, the head of the logging company, very angry. He was jealous. Insanely jealous, some say.

"The rivalry between the two became heated. They started recruiting each other's workers, offering higher pay and benefits. Anything to stifle the other's business."

"What does this have to do with the old truck and all this ghost stuff I've been seeing?" Zach asked.

"Patience, son. Patience," Miranda said calmly before returning to her story. "Even though the rivalry had become ugly, the real drama began on the day of the fire. It was early in the morning and Victor Leppla's son, Kristian, drove to the logging plant in his family's old pickup truck. Kristian handled many of the day-to-day operations of the business and he was almost always the first one to work in the morning. "Unfortunately for him, while he was working, a fire broke out. Keep in mind, this was a logging plant, so the fire had plenty of fuel. It spread quickly. Kristian had no chance. He was tragically killed that day."

"So, is it Kristian out there haunting these woods?" Zach asked.

"Just hold on now," Miranda said. "To this day no one knows how that fire got started, but Victor Leppla was certain Fredrik Sutinen had something to do with it. But here's where the story really gets interesting. Rumor has it that Victor was more than just a businessman. Some say he had certain powers."

"What kind of powers?"

"Are you sure you want to know?" Miranda asked.

"Yes, you gotta tell me now!"

Miranda moved closer to Zach, putting her face close to his. She looked into his eyes. "Witch powers," she said.

Zach scooted away from Miranda.

"People used to see him doing all sorts of strange things on his land. Things that couldn't be explained. There were claims of strange lights glowing from within his home. He put an addition on his wood cabin. Some say it was used for some pretty creepy stuff. Neighbors complained of the strange smell emitted from the smoke in his chimney. Who knows what he was doing in there?"

Zach remembered the odd smell that had been following him. "But the story doesn't end there."

"Why? What happened next?" Zach asked eagerly.

"When Kristian was killed, Victor placed a curse on the Sutinen family."

"A curse? You've got to be kidding me. There's no such thing."

"Think about it, Zach. Do you really believe that? If so, then why did you come to me in the cafeteria today?"

Zach looked down at his feet.

"Victor didn't just put a curse on the Sutinen family. The legend has it that Mr. Leppla stood in the middle of the town square, with hundreds of people watching, and vowed to haunt this area for eternity . . . even after his own death."

"So, is this a legend, or is this true?"

"What do you think?" asked Miranda.

Zach ran through all the images in his head: the truck, the mysterious figure in the woods, the glowing, the smell. "Ok, so let's say this is all true. Victor is out there haunting these woods. He put a curse on the Sutinens. How do you know so much about it if everyone else thinks it's just a story?"

Miranda stared silently at Zach for a moment. Speaking softly, she said, "Like I said before, this story has had life around these parts for a long time."

"Yeah, but how do you know it isn't just an old ghost story, used to scare kids like me when they come up to Pine Ridge?"

"Because I heard this story long before I came to work at Pine Ridge."

"What do you mean?" Zach asked.

"The Sutinen and Leppla families have been telling this story for many, many years, Zach."

"Okay, so . . ."

"My name is Miranda, Zach. Miranda . . . Leppla."

Chapter 7

"VICTOR LEPPLA WAS MY GRANDFATHER," Miranda explained. "He died when I was still a little girl, so my memories of him are cloudy. My father was Kristian's little brother, Mikko."

"Oh, my God." Zach was in shock. He gathered himself and said, "How did Victor die?"

"Supposedly, it was a heart attack."

"You don't think that's true?"

"I'm not sure. He never had any health problems as far as I know. It has always seemed weird to me that he would have died that way. There's something fishy about that story, if you ask me." Miranda scooted away from Zach. Her fingers tapped her right knee incessantly. "My parents tried to hide the family secret from me for a long time. But I heard all the rumors anyway. They just wouldn't confirm any of them.

"We moved away from this area to live in Missouri. But when I got older something called me back to these woods. I needed to know the truth about my grandpa. So, when Pine Ridge opened, I became the head cook and I've been here ever since."

"How did you find out the truth about your grandpa if your parents never told you?"

Miranda's fingers stopped tapping. She stared deeply into Zach's anxious eyes. "Because he told me."

A shiver traveled up Zach's spine. "What do you mean, 'he told you'? I thought he was dead."

"He was dead . . . He is dead. But that didn't stop him from coming to me. He told me everything. Zach, he wanted a partner. Someone to help him carry out his curse. Someone from the living world."

"What did you do?"

"Nothing, Zach. I wouldn't join him. And now . . . now he won't leave me alone. Those things you talked about: the truck, the glowing, the smell. I know all about them because I see them too. More than you know."

Zach leaned back on the bench. He gave a heavy sigh. "Miranda?"

Miranda was silent.

"What does this have to do with me? Why do I keep seeing these things? What does he want with me?"

Miranda shook her head slowly. "That one you'll have to find out for yourself, Zach."

The campfire crowd was making their way up the path toward Zach and Miranda.

Miranda stood up, patted Zach on his left shoulder and before walking back to the cafeteria, said, "You find the answer, Zach. You find out."

ZACH CRAWLED INTO THE top bunk with no intention of falling asleep. His mind was racing. Logan was below him, engrossed in a book. He had a reading light attached to the pages, which he never left home without. There was no talking to Logan when he was reading. Michael and Tristan had already closed their eyes.

It was 10:00 P.M. Time for lights out. Zach could hear Mr. Loeb and Mr. Foster whispering outside their door. Zach would not be sleeping anytime soon. "Logan," Zach whispered, peering over the edge of the bunk.

"What?" Logan responded, not taking his eyes off the book.

"Will you go into my bag and toss me my phone?"

"What are you gonna do with that right now?"

"Don't worry about it. Just give it to me, will you?"

"You'd better not get caught with it. You'll get it taken away. Or, who knows? You might get sent home."

There was only one rule about having cell phones at Pine Ridge:

You Don't Have Them. Under no circumstances were any students to be using their phones on this trip. For the most part, people had complied, but Zach was about to break yet another rule.

Logan handed Zach his iPhone.

Miranda's story seemed real enough. Why would she make something up like that? But like she said, Zach had to find out for himself. Were Victor Leppla and Fredrik Sutinen real people? Was Victor Leppla really a witch? And what did it have to do with him? He hoped to find out through the magic of Google.

The screen on his phone glowed as he opened Safari and typed in the two rivals' names. When the "hits" appeared he studied the key words: "logging," "Finland," "Business," "Mayor." Everything he saw confirmed Miranda's story.

He scrolled down toward the bottom of the page. The words, "fire" and "feud" appeared. But just as he was going to click on the link, a knock came at the door. He hastily tucked his phone under his sleeping bag and closed his eyes. He heard Logan doing the same with his book. Mr. Loeb poked his head into the room, saw that everyone was sleeping, and quietly closed the door behind him.

Zach turned on his phone again, peering at it under his sleeping bag. He clicked on the link and read. It described the history of Finland, Minnesota in detail. It looked credible enough to Zach. It even had black and white pictures of log cabins and old cars. It was history.

But one thing was missing, it made no mention of Victor Leppla being a witch or cursing the Sutinen family.

Zach made a new Google search for "Victor Leppla witch". He finished typing the words in the search box and hit "enter."

Blackness.

The screen had disappeared as if the battery had suddenly died. He had charged his phone before the trip and this was the first time he had used it. There was no way the battery could be dead.

He tried to turn the phone on again, but with no luck.

Zach put the phone down and plugged his nose. The stench had returned. The same odor that had assaulted his senses when he stepped off the bus. Gasoline. Burnt rubber. It was nauseating. He leaned over the top of his bunk to check with Logan, but he was already fast asleep. Michael and Tristan snored rhythmically across the room.

Zach quickly climbed down the ladder of his bed. He rifled through his overnight bag and found the jeans he had worn before he went to bed. He stuck his hand in the right pocket and snatched Chris's stone. With it firmly in one fist, he climbed back up to the top bunk, crawled into his sleeping bag, and lay on his back, staring wide-eyed at the ceiling, the gem firmly against his heart.

Eventually the stench faded away, leaving Zach in peace.

ZACH BARELY SLEPT. His grip on Chris's rock stayed firm throughout the night, but every creak of a door opening, every brush of the leaves woke him. His mind raced. His heart pounded.

Through the window dawn beckoned beyond the dense forest, waking the crisp Minnesota morning. Zach groggily climbed down the ladder of his bunk.

Logan still slept soundly.

"Logan," Zach whispered, trying to wake him. "Hey, Logan," he called again. Logan turned on his side, pulling the covers tighter over his body. Zach gave up trying to rouse him from his sleep.

He set the stone down carefully next to his bag, slid off his pajamas, and put on a pair of jeans and his Minnesota Timberwolves hoodie. He jammed his Twins hat on to his bare head and, hoping Logan would wake up, sat on the end of Logan's bed to put on his socks and tennis shoes. It was unsuccessful. Logan was still asleep, drooling profusely on his pillow.

Logan was sound asleep, but Michael and Tristan's beds were empty, both of their sleeping bags rolled up tidily. *They must have gotten up early to check out more nature stuff*, Zach thought.

Zach bent over and grabbed the stone from the floor. Then he stuffed it into his front pocket and walked to the lobby.

He was alone. Everyone else in the building was sleeping, including Mr. Loeb, Mr. Foster, and Mr. Preston. Zach pushed open the door and stepped outside into the chilly morning air. He scanned the area for life. Two Pine Ridge employees were walking towards the cafeteria across from the dorm. Was it Miranda? Zach looked more closely. The two workers were taller than Miranda and didn't hunch over as they walked. "We have Kitchen Patrol tonight," Zach remembered out loud. "I bet Miranda will be there."

Zach stood on the sidewalk, which led to the campfire pit. Along the path were four benches. Two on each side of the path. This was where he and Miranda had spoken the night before. He found the same bench and sat down.

There was no sign of Michael and Tristan.

Zach breathed in the fresh, cool air, and watched the bright sun rising in the distance above the green forest. No foul odor this morning. No strange figures in the woods. If a ghost haunted Pine Ridge, it was not evident then. For just a brief moment, Zach forgot about Victor Leppla, forgot about his mom's threat to send him to his dad's, and he even forgot about Chris . . . just for a brief moment.

He sat in peace for fifteen minutes when the cabin door opened. Mr. Foster stepped outside, put his hands on his hips, and took a deep breath, soaking in the clean, brisk air. "You're up awfully early," he called to Zach.

"Yeah, I couldn't sleep last night."

Mr. Foster sauntered over to the bench and sat down next to him, staring at the forested hills. "Is something bothering you? Is that why you couldn't sleep?"

Zach was silent for a moment, gathering his thoughts. "There's a bunch of stuff I guess."

"What kind of stuff?" he asked, probing.

"My mom told me that if I didn't behave on this trip and get my grades up when we get back, I'd have to go live with my dad."

"Where does your dad live?"

"Two Harbors. We passed it on the way up here."

"Yeah, I know where it is. It's a nice town," said Mr. Foster. "So, I'm guessing moving to Two Harbors is not your first choice?"

"No, not at all. I mean, I love my dad, but after Chris disappeared, he just took off. He's kept in touch, but after my parents' divorce, he felt this sudden need to move up here. Something about being closer to the crime scene. He got a teaching job at a college in Duluth. I don't understand it and I don't want to move."

Mr. Foster nodded, his eyes squinting a bit, showing their concern. He paused for a moment. "Zach, you're a really smart kid. You're more than capable of getting those grades up. With everything you've been through, I completely understand why your academics have taken a back seat. Losing your brother, your parents getting divorced. That would be tough on anyone, especially a fourteen-year-old boy."

Zach put his head down, staring at the ground.

"But you still have choices to make. You have choices to make on the rest of this trip. You have choices to make when you return home. I can't decide what will happen with your situation. Whether you move to your dad's is a decision your parents will need to make, but I do know you have the opportunity to make smart choices from here on out. You can't change what has already happened. That stunt you pulled at the ropes course . . . I'm not sure what you were thinking, but it's over. You need to focus only on what's ahead of you. And as far as I'm concerned, you have a very bright future. So, remember that, okay?"

Zach looked up from the ground, made eye contact with Mr. Foster, and then looked out at the trees again, nodding in agreement.

"Zach? Could you tell me about Chris? I'd love to hear about him," said Mr. Foster.

Zach didn't answer. Silent, he stared into the wilderness.

"Okay. Maybe some other time. Whenever you're ready." Mr. Foster patted Zach on the knee, stood up from the bench and walked up the sidewalk toward the dorm.

"He was kind of nerdy," Zach called after Mr. Foster.

Mr. Foster stopped, turned around, and waited for Zach to continue.

"He was kind of nerdy, but he was also the nicest kid I've ever known."

Mr. Foster came back and sat down next to Zach again.

"We were really different. He was always into the science and math stuff and I was the athlete. We still got along pretty well I guess. But, I could have treated him better. He would get picked on sometimes and I knew it, but I didn't stick up for him like I should have." Zach still didn't make eye contact with Mr. Foster. Instead, he spoke to the trees, the breeze, and the crisp morning air. "I wish I could have been there for him when he went missing. I wish I could have stopped it."

Mr. Foster put his hand on Zach's shoulder. The two sat on the bench in silence for what felt like a lifetime.

The sun had made its way above the tips of the trees and students had started to amble out of the dorm, making their way to the cafeteria for breakfast.

"Thanks for sharing that with me, Zach," said Mr. Foster as he stood and prepared to join the others en route.

Zach stood up from the bench and quickly scanned the group of students moving toward breakfast, looking for Michael and Tristan. "Hey, Mr. Foster!" he yelled.

"Yeah, Zach?"

"Have you seen Michael or Tristan around? They weren't in their beds when I got up and I haven't seen them since."

"No, I haven't, but I am sure they're around. Let's check at the cafeteria, okay?"

"Okay." Zach stuffed his cold hands in his pockets and made his way toward the cafeteria. This time he wasn't alone. Logan had joined him, walking in rhythm.

After breakfast the students gathered once again in front of the campfire pit. Zach examined the crowd, looking for Michael and Tristan. He hadn't seen them at breakfast. Logan and Jenny stood next to him. "Hey, have you two seen Michael and Tristan? I haven't seen them all morning," Zach asked.

"I saw 'em," Jenny said.

"You did? Where?"

"Right there!" She smiled and pointed down the gravel trail. Michael and Tristan were jogging towards the group, breathing heavily.

"Where have you two been?" asked Mrs. Lomeier.

"We . . . are . . . really . . . sorry," replied Michael, gasping for air between his words. "Tristan and I got up real early to do some exploring on our own and we kind of lost track of time. We're real sorry, Mrs. Lomeier."

"Well, okay, but we will have to discuss this later," Mrs. Lomeier said. Her tone was less condescending than it had been with Zach.

As the groups were breaking up to go to their classes, Zach approached Michael and Tristan. "Where did you guys go? We had no idea where you were."

Both boys looked shocked at Zach's concern. "We just went down the big staircase and into the woods. We wanted to see some animals. It's easier to do if you don't have as many people around," said Michael.

"Yeah, and I wanted to find some more rocks to keep," added Tristan.

Zach pictured Chris searching for his "perfect rocks."

"All right," Zach said. "You should probably tell someone before you do something like that though."

Michael and Tristan looked at each other curiously.

Zach found his way back to Logan and Jenny. Tanya had also joined them. He turned back to the two boys. "Oh, by the way, did you happen to see any pickup trucks down there?"

"What do you mean?" asked Tristan.

Michael just shook his head.

"Nothing. Never mind."

The rest of the day was relatively uneventful. The students learned about birds, plants and teamwork. Speaking to Mr. Foster had made Zach feel a little better. Logan was the only person he had ever spoken to about Chris's disappearance. He wasn't sure what had compelled him to share with Mr. Foster, but it felt good.

Zach remembered what Mr. Foster had said about making choices. It was true. He couldn't control anything in the past, but he could control how he approached the present. He hadn't encountered any ghostly images or strange occurrences all day. *There are no such things as ghosts,* he thought to himself. Miranda must have been putting him on. He was going to enjoy the rest of the fieldtrip. He wasn't going to get into any more trouble. He would deal with the situation with his mom when he got home. Those were the only choices he could make. He was sure of it.

By the end of the day, he was back to wrestling with Logan and joking about him and Jenny. He was even joking about kitchen patrol duty that night. "You better check your dinner tonight. Who knows what I might do to it," Zach told Adam and Mitch.

The old Zach had returned.

At least for the moment.

But that evening, KP duty turned out to be no laughing matter for Zach. The haunting was only just beginning.

Chapter 8

STUDENTS WHO HAD KP were to arrive at the cafeteria thirty minutes before mealtime to eat and receive instructions. Zach arrived a few minutes early, along with Logan, Michael and Tristan. He hadn't told the others, but he wanted a chance to see Miranda before the rest of the students arrived.

Zach led the other three into the kitchen.

Miranda was waiting for them. "Welcome, kids. I'm Miranda. I'll be helping you through your KP duty tonight." She avoided eye contact with Zach, speaking only to the others. "We'll wait a couple of minutes for everyone to get here, then I'll go through your instructions."

Zach felt awkward now. Why was Miranda ignoring him?

A group of four girls also had duty. They entered the kitchen shortly after Zach, Logan, Michael and Tristan. Zach knew that the tall, brown-haired girl's name was Brittany, only because she played basketball and Zach would sometimes see her playing before or after his own games. The other three he had seen around school, but didn't know their names.

Once all the students were present, Miranda began. She spoke directly and with authority. There was an efficient way to do things in the kitchen and Miranda was there to make sure it happened. But still she did not look Zach in the eye.

Miranda asked every student to introduce him or herself. The three girls Zach didn't know were named Elsie, Shanda and Mariah.

Zach and Elsie were appointed the job of food servers. Shanda, Logan, Brittany and Kayla were the dishwashers, and the undesirable job of "food waste patrols" went to Mariah and Michael. They had to watch every trash can and then weigh the waste at the end of the evening. KP was a well-oiled machine with Miranda at the helm.

The responsibilities had been divided up and everyone made their way to their assigned posts. But before the crowd of students rolled in to get their food, Zach wanted to talk to Miranda. He found her at the back of the kitchen, alone, prepping the dishwasher. "Miranda?"

She turned around. "Yes?"

"You were just messin' with me last night, right? That whole thing about Victor- it's all just a story, isn't it?" Zach whispered.

"Son, I don't know what you mean. But I do know there is a lot of work to do, so you had better head back to your post. The other children will be here soon." Miranda walked away from Zach. She moved to the other side of the kitchen to wipe down a countertop. As she bent over to rub the worktop, she tilted her head toward Zach, opened her eyes wide, and shook her head at him slightly.

Zach walked to his food-serving station. Miranda didn't want to answer his questions. Not here anyway. Not now. But why?

Maybe she was telling the truth after all.

With hairnets and plastic gloves on, Elsie handed each student a crispy grilled cheese sandwich, while Zach dished up a ladle of chicken noodle soup. Adam held out his tray to Zach. "Serve me!" he said mockingly.

Zach handed him the bowl, not acknowledging Adam's joke.

The end of the line was in sight. Just three hungry, antsy students remained. Zach peered into the soup kettle, making sure there was enough for the three students to have their share. Serving soup for the past twenty minutes, Zach had grown accustomed to the familiar smell. But when Zach stuck his nose into the kettle to check its contents, this time it emitted a different, all too familiar odor. Gasoline mixed with burnt rubber. It was unmistakable.

Zach jumped back, knocking over the kettle of soup. The soup spilled over the counter and dripped down on to the floor in front of him, startling Elsie and the other students in line.

"What happened?" asked Elsie. Zach stared at the soup on the floor, not responding to the question. "Zach, you okay?"

"Did you smell that?"

"Smell what? The soup?" Elsie was confused.

"No, not the soup. It was something totally different. I've smelled it a few times since we've been here. A smell like burnt rubber and gasoline. You really didn't smell that?"

Elsie and the students in line shook their heads.

Zach looked over to see Logan standing next to him with damp dishrags in his hands.

"Thanks, man," Zach said. "Here give me a rag." Zach got down on his knees along with Logan, wiping up the spilled soup. "I smelled that weird odor again and it freaked me out."

"What odor? What are you talking about?" asked Logan.

"Remember, when we got off the bus? I asked you if you smelled it then."

"Oh, yeah. Do you still smell it now?"

"No, not anymore. It just comes real quick and then it's gone." Zach felt stupid trying to explain it, even to Logan.

Logan lifted the empty soup kettle back on to the counter and took the dirty rags to the sink to wash them out.

Zach breathed deeply. When he was on the pitching mound, deep breathing always helped him get through the tough innings. It helped him refocus. Elsie looked over at him, smiling. *Everything is fine*, he thought. The odor is in my imagination. It doesn't mean anything.

The three students left in line had disappeared. Elsie began to clean up her grilled cheese station. Zach did the same with his soup kettle.

Looking out over the cafeteria full of middle schoolers, Zach grabbed the handles of the soup kettle, expecting it to be lightweight and empty. But it wasn't. He could hardly lift it. Once again, he peered into the kettle. This time he didn't have to look all the way to the bottom. The soup was nearly overflowing. The kettle was filled to the rim, just as it had been when he began the evening. It was as if Zach hadn't dished out a single spoonful.

Shaking his head in confusion, Zach backed up slowly, running into the wall behind him.

"Are you okay?" Elsie asked.

"The kettle is full again," he responded, still staring at the soup kettle.

"What do you mean, 'again?' We just started serving. It's supposed to be full."

Zach's head shot up. A line of students waiting to receive food overflowed into the lobby of the cafeteria. The tables of the cafeteria were empty. Logan, Shanda, Brittany and Tristan stood toward the back of the kitchen, waiting for dirty dishes to clean. Elsie's tray was full of grilled cheese, enough for all thirty campers. No one had eaten yet. The soup had not been spilled.

Zach had gone back in time.

It was as if the last twenty minutes of his life had never happened and he seemed to be the only one aware of it.

He just stood there. Either he was going crazy, or he *was* being haunted. The pickup truck, the shadowy images, the glowing lights, the smell. They weren't figments of his imagination. Miranda must have been telling the truth. He was sure of it now.

Something was out there playing with him like a toy, and for whatever reason, it wasn't going to leave him alone.

Chapter 9

ZACH PUT DOWN HIS soup ladle, took off his hairnet, gloves and apron and rushed to the back of the kitchen. "Miranda? Miranda?"

Miranda was nowhere to be found.

Zach found another kitchen employee who was helping clean pots and pans. She was tall and thin. Much younger than Miranda. "Excuse me. I don't feel well. I think I might throw up. I need to go to the bathroom." He was only half lying.

"Okay, just go! Hurry!" the woman said. "I'll take over your post. Don't worry."

Zach rushed out of the kitchen, the rest of the KP staff watching him intently, including Logan.

Once outside, the pine and spruce trees seemed to cave in on Zach. The circular shape of the camp turned him in circles. Since everyone was in the cafeteria, he was alone, standing in the middle of the camp, like the bull's eye on a dartboard. Whatever was after him would have no problem getting to him here. He was vulnerable. Defenseless.

He grabbed Chris's stone from his pocket and raced to the dormitory front door, his feet barely grazing the gravel below.

Where had Miranda gone?

He sat on the floor of his room, his back planted against the wall. He held the rock in his hands, twirling it, studying its grainy texture and flawed shape. The perfect stone. Chris's perfect stone.

With every rustle of trees in the cool breeze and with every click-clack of a squirrel's footsteps, Zach jumped nervously. What was after him? What did it want from him? Zach was lost. He didn't know what to do.

A few minutes passed. A slow creaking came from the lobby of the dorm. Zach stood up, the stone still firmly in his hand. The creaking became louder with each passing second. Louder. Louder. Zach's eyes were wide. A chill ran up his spine. Then the door slowly opened. He shrunk against the stiffness of the wall behind him. "Leave me alone!" he yelled.

"Zach, it's Mr. Foster. Are you okay?"

Zach's muscles relaxed. A deep breath released from his mouth. "Yeah, Mr. Foster. I'm okay."

"The lady from the cafeteria said you had to leave because you felt sick. Is that true?"

"Uh, yeah. I was feeling a little nauseous, so I had to get out and get some fresh air."

"Okay, but you know you aren't supposed to be in here by yourself right now."

Zach shrugged.

"Are you sure there isn't something else going on?"

The chatter of fifteen eighth graders coming back to the dorm interrupted the conversation. "No, I'm fine."

"All right. So, you're ready to go out on the night hike then?"

"Yeah, I'll be ready for it," Zach said.

The night hike was almost as famous as the Ropes Course at Pine Ridge. Mrs. Lomeier had told Zach's class all about it. After dinner the entire group of campers would gather together at the campfire pit. Then Mrs. Lomeier would lead the kids down the path into the deep forest.

Mrs. Lomeier stressed two things about the night hike. "Always follow the person in front of you and don't ever stray from the path." She was paranoid about losing students in the woods.

Mr. Foster left Zach's room, but as soon as he was gone, Logan, Michael and Tristan entered. "Hey. You all right?" Logan asked.

"Yeah. I'm fine." He looked at Michael and Tristan, hastily putting on extra layers for the chilly excursion. "I'll talk to you later about it."

"Okay," said Logan.

Michael and Tristan finished putting on their hats, gloves, and heavy coats for the adventure. "You guys coming?" asked Tristan excitedly.

"Yeah. We'll meet you guys out there," Logan said as the two friends dashed out the door. "So, what's going on with you? How come you darted out of KP duty? Were you actually sick?"

Zach shoved the stone back into his pocket. He turned around to look out at the dimming daylight. The sun was casting shadows among the dense trees. Soon it would be dark. Soon it would be night.

Still staring out the window, Zach asked, "Would you believe me if I told you?"

Logan was silent for a moment. Then he said honestly, "Yeah. I'll believe you."

Zach sat on Logan's bed with a somber look on his face, told him about the terrible odor, the soup spilling and then reappearing, him going back in time, and Miranda's story. He tossed it all out there for Logan, expecting him to laugh. Expecting him to blow it off.

"So, you think this place really is haunted and ghosts are after you?"

"Yeah. I do."

"You're full of it. You've never believed in this kind of stuff before."

Zach just stared at Logan, saying nothing.

"You're serious, aren't you?"

"I wish it wasn't real. Trust me. But after the KP incident, it has to be true."

Logan nodded, affirming Zach's story. "Okay. What can I do?"

Zach stood up, went to his overnight bag, and pulled out his winter layers. He took off his Twins hat and replaced it with a warm, knit stocking cap. Then he put on his gloves. He turned, looking directly into Logan's eyes. "There's only one thing you can do."

"What's that?"

"On this night hike?"

"Yeah?"

"Don't leave me."

Chapter 10

ZACH FELT CAGED BY the sheer darkness of the path and the woods. The students surrounding him were giddy with laughter and excitement, but he felt none of that. Mrs. Lomeier's flashlight was carving through the blackness at the front of the group, while Mr. Loeb's light shined from the rear. Though Zach couldn't see his face, Logan was safely by his side.

Every footstep in leaves, every chirping bird, every time another student jumped out from behind a tree, Zach's heart skipped. It was unfamiliar territory for him. He wasn't afraid of anything, at least not until now. Something was going to happen on this hike. He was sure of it.

Every once in a while Logan would nudge Zach's arm and ask, "You all right?"

Zach would lie and say, "Yeah, I'm fine."

They walked for a while over small, rolling hills, climbing over the occasional log blocking the path.

Zach was relieved when they reached the end of the hike.

None of the teachers had disclosed the "secret destination" of the hike. It was a surprise. At the end of the path there was a dim light. For the first time, Zach and the other students could see the ground they were walking on. The path led directly to a pile of boulders. To reach the "secret destination" the students would have to climb the giant rocks. Zach was thrilled to be out of the blackness, so he ran to the front of the line and climbed the stone wall first.

Logan followed closely behind.

When they reached the summit, the source of the dim light became clear. It was like nothing Zach had ever seen. Although it was nearly 9:00 at night, the vast sky provided a respite from the constant darkness. Bright, sparkling stars smothered the atmosphere.

"I've never seen so many stars in my life," Logan said, gazing at the sky, his mouth wide open.

Zach was silent, taking in the spectacle.

They were standing on a giant rock formation. It had a fairly smooth surface, and was set at a slight incline- perfect for lying down and staring up at the night sky.

"Everyone look out to the horizon," called Mrs. Lomeier. "Do you see that big, dark area of nothingness?"

A few students nodded, while the others scanned the area Mrs. Lomeier had indicated.

"It's actually not 'nothing.' That's Lake Superior. It's about five miles from here and it looks just like a black hole in the dark, doesn't it?"

After a few minutes of "oohing" and "ahhing" the students followed the teachers' leads as they lay down to soak in the stars' glow.

Mrs. Lomeier whispered to any student who'd listen. She pointed out every constellation she could find. Otherwise, the group was quiet.

Zach lay next to Logan. Jenny and Tanya had caught up to them and were lying on Logan's right side. Zach stared at the stars intently, thinking about his brother. Was he up there among the stars? Would Zach be joining him someday? It was this thought that brought him back to his immediate reality. Maybe the hauntings he had experienced were a clue to answering this question. Maybe he would be joining Chris sooner than he expected and sooner than he wanted.

Zach suddenly jumped to his feet. He had let his guard down. Whatever was out there haunting him had had a chance to do whatever it wanted. He wouldn't let that happen again.

Logan stood up with him. "What's wrong? Did you see something again?" he asked.

"No. But something could happen at any time."

"What's going on?" Jenny asked. She and Tanya had followed Logan's lead and stood together.

"Nothing," Zach replied quickly, not allowing Logan to elaborate in any way. "I just got tired of lying there." The momentary peace Zach experienced under the serenity of the stars was gone. He walked down the slope of the rock. The glow of the stars was not as bright here. Dark shadows surrounded him.

The other students had begun to rise and chatter behind him.

At the bottom of the giant stone surface was blackness. Zach inched closer to what he presumed was a steep drop off. The farther he moved down the slope, the darker it got. The line between the rock he was standing on and the forest below was no longer clearly defined. He dug his feet into the hardness of the stone to keep his balance. Then he carefully peered over the edge. The land fell away from the rock into a black abyss. Zach snapped his head back to maintain his hold on the rock. Once he stabilized himself, he looked to the stars.

Zach overheard Mrs. Lomeier telling some students about the constellation *Perseus*. He'd read the story of the ancient Greek hero in English class. He scanned the sky. The outline of the legendary figure became clear, defined. Holding the head of Medusa, Perseus showed his strength and confidence. His power seemed to radiate throughout the dark atmosphere.

Zach gazed at the powerful figure, sensing his courage. He leaned back and sat on the rock, still staring at the image of Perseus. He braced himself by planting his hands on the stone behind him.

The longer he stared, the brighter Perseus became. The brilliance of the constellation seemed to energize Zach.

He stood again and clamped his hands together. His grip was strong and firm. Perseus was there for him. Telling him something.

Zach closed his eyes. He imagined Perseus speaking to him. "You are strong," he would say. "You are a warrior."

Zach opened his eyes and looked up at the hero. Then he spun around to find his classmates mingling with each other. He took in a deep breath and turned to face Perseus one last time. The bright outline was even easier to see now.

Zach thought about the pickup truck. He pondered the odor and strange images he had seen in the woods. He thought about Miranda's story. And he thought about Victor Leppla.

Before joining his friends, he took in one more deep breath. Then, slowly and confidently, he looked up at Perseus . . . and nodded.

As Zach made his way back through the woods with Logan by his side, his senses somehow seemed keener, more defined.

Halfway up the trail, Mitch and Adam jumped out from behind a tree and yelled, "Hey!" Logan almost jumped out of his skin in fright, but Zach barely flinched. He gave only a slight smile, appreciating the prank. The noises, the smells, and the visions no longer frightened him as they had on the first leg of the hike. Now he was intensely aware, ready for whatever was to happen.

He followed the glow of Mrs. Lomeier's flashlight, carefully stepping over logs and stones when necessary. He imagined himself as Perseus, carrying the head of Medusa, bravely flaunting his trophy.

The trees at the trail end opened in welcoming fashion. Lights in the buildings of Pine Ridge guided Zach and the others back to the campfire pit. He sat on one of the benches, watching Logan and Jenny flirt. Nothing happened, he thought. Victor never showed up. What's he waiting for?

Adam and Mitch were running around tackling each other.

The last of the group wandered up to the campfire pit, Mr. Loeb's light bringing up the rear.

"Okay, kids. Let's take a quick attendance to make sure we didn't lose anyone out there, and then we can head off to bed," said Mrs. Lomeier. She began listing off students' names according to cabin assignments. "Zach Sutton?" she called.

"Here," Zach said calmly.

"Logan Goldsmith?"

"Here."

"Michael Tynes?" No answer. Mrs. Lomeier scanned the crowd. "Michael Tynes!" she repeated more loudly. Still no answer. She gave a look to the other teachers that seemed to say, "Look for him."

As Mr. Foster, Mr. Loeb and the others browsed through the crowd looking for Michael, Mrs. Lomeier continued. "Tristan Phillips?" No answer. "Tristan Phillips!" Again, no answer. A murmur resonated through the crowd.

"Mr. Foster," Zach called.

"Yes, Zach?" Mr. Foster was searching, his eyes showing concern.

"Where are Michael and Tristan?"

"Don't worry, Zach. I'm sure they're around here somewhere."

Logan left Jenny and found Zach. "Where are they?" Logan asked.

"I don't know," Zach said.

"Maybe they're just looking for rocks or animals again."

"It's pitch dark out here."

Logan didn't reply.

Zach began scouring the crowd.

The other students weren't overly concerned. "I bet they're hiding somewhere," Tanya said.

Mrs. Pliska was circling the nearby woods, carrying Mrs. Lomeier's flashlight. "Any sign of them, Mrs. Pliska?" Zach asked.

"Afraid not. But they're around here somewhere. Why don't you just head back with your friends, okay?"

Zach found his way back to Logan, who was talking with Jenny. "I think they're gone," he said matter of factly.

"I bet they'll turn up," Jenny said.

Logan didn't respond.

"Okay, everyone. Listen up!" Mrs. Lomeier yelled. "All of you are going to head back to your cabins now. I know some of you are concerned about Michael and Tristan, but we'll handle it. They've got to be around here somewhere. When we find them we'll let you know."

Zach and Logan were back in their room, two bunk beds emptier. "Something happened," said Zach. "There is no way this is a coincidence."

"What do you mean?"

"You know what I mean. All these things I've been seeing. Michael and Tristan disappearing. They're related."

"You don't know that for sure. Michael and Tristan were missing this morning too and they made it back fine."

Zach reached into his pocket and pulled out the stone.

"What's that?" asked Logan.

Before Zach had a chance to answer, Mr. Foster poked his head into the room. "Hey guys. How are you doing?"

"Did you find 'em?" Zach asked.

"I haven't heard anything yet, but they're still looking. Hang in there, okay guys? We'll let you know when we figure this out."

"Okay, thanks," Logan said as Mr. Foster closed the door behind him.

"They aren't going to find 'em," said Zach.

"You don't know that. Come on. Let's go to sleep and I bet when we wake up, Michael and Tristan will be sleeping in their beds."

Zach clutched the stone in his hand, climbed up to his bed, and laid his head on his pillow. He did not close his eyes. Instead, he grabbed the edge of his sleeping bag and covered his nose with it.

The stench had returned. Gasoline and burnt rubber. This was all too familiar.

He released the sleeping bag and took Chris's stone in both of his hands. He gripped it as hard as he could, feeling the imprint of the gritty surface on his palms.

Logan was quiet below. He could always fall asleep quickly.

As the odor penetrated, Zach sat up in his bed. He felt strength in his hands, in his heart. The strength of Perseus. The strength of Chris.

He jammed the stone back into his pocket and quietly climbed down to the floor. He put on his shoes. He put on his jacket and warm hat, while Logan snored softly. The empty bunk beds across the room silently asked for help. The teachers didn't know what they were dealing with. They would never find Michael and Tristan.

Zach opened the door to peek into the hall. Silent. No one around. He opened the door fully and tiptoed out of the room. He crept through the lobby, opened the door, and snuck out into the crisp night air.

The campus was dark and eerily silent. Lights shone through the windows of the administrative building. It was across the gravel path, but Zach could see Mrs. Lomeier and Mr. Loeb standing in the window. Mrs. Lomeier was on the phone, pacing.

Pine Ridge was vast. He wasn't sure where he was going or where he should look, but Michael and Tristan were somewhere out there. And Zach was the only one who could find them.

PART 2

Chapter 11

ZACH HAD BEEN HIKING FOR NEARLY AN HOUR. He had decided to begin his search on the same path from which Michael and Tristan had disappeared. The night hike path.

The moonlight breeched the trees and found the surface of an old log on the side of the trail. Zach sat on the log, resting his rubbery legs.

He had not come prepared. No flashlight. No food. No water. And now he was lost. The hike earlier that night did not take nearly this long. He must have taken a wrong turn in the darkness. How could he be so stupid?

The silence of the woods was chilling. Occasionally a soft breeze would rustle the leaves and remind Zach that he had not been sucked into a dark, cavernous, vacuum. Hunger had started to creep into his belly, dryness into his throat.

He worried. What have I done? I have no idea where Michael and Tristan are and now I have no idea where I am.

Looking around, he searched for any clue as to his whereabouts. Any clue that could lead him to the comfort of his bed. To food. To water. To Michael and Tristan.

The moon emitted enough light to outline the boundaries of the path. This was Zach's only guide. His only beacon. In a strange way, he almost wanted the ghost to make its presence known again. At least then he wouldn't feel so alone. He wouldn't feel so lost.

In Zach's first class at Pine Ridge, Melanie had mentioned that all of the myriad trails in the Pine Ridge area were interconnected. That if you ever got lost, the best thing you could do would be to stay on the paths. If you did that, rather than venturing into the woods, you would stand a much better chance of finding civilization.

Keeping this advice in mind, he rose from the surface of the log, took a deep breath, and made his way along the path, back the way he came.

ZACH'S TOES AND FINGERTIPS were numb. In his hurry to escape the dorm, he had forgotten to put on his gloves and his snow boots. All the students were told to bring boots just in case, but it had not been snowing, so Zach was wearing his Nikes. Since he had left the dorm two hours earlier the temperature had dropped and he could feel it in his bones.

The path had become nearly invisible in the dark. Black clouds smothered the remaining moonlight. Zach had to hike slowly and carefully just to stay on the trail. He tripped over rocks and even his own feet.

Walking down the path took every ounce of his effort. He had never before felt such hunger and thirst. He walked with his mouth open, hoping the cool breeze would give his throat some relief.

Not seeing a comfortable place to sit, he crouched down in the middle of the dirt path and put his face in his hands. Tears welled up in his eyes. Zach couldn't cry at Chris's memorial, but he had no trouble doing it now.

When he finally eased to his feet, small, white flakes had begun to coat the trail and the surrounding trees. "Great! That's just what I need!" he yelled to the sky. But his anger quickly dispelled. He had an idea. On a nearby pine tree, a patch of snow lay on the branches, leftover from previous snowfalls. Zach walked over to it, grabbed a handful, and nibbled on the wet, cool slush. It was dirty. Who knew how long it had been sitting on the branch. But it eased the pain in Zach's throat.

Zach trudged forward along the trail. He had to keep moving to stay warm. It would be hours before daylight showed its face. He had almost forgotten why he was out there in the first place. All he could think about was getting back to the dorm, getting warm, and eating.

The soft, slow snowfall created an eerie quiet. The flakes were larger and falling at an increasingly fast rate. "I'm never gonna be able to see this trail if the ground is covered in snow." Zach stopped in his tracks.

He turned in every direction, calming himself. "Okay. I can figure this out. I've been in jams before. I can get back. Just stay calm."

Just as Zach was beginning to find his bearings, a breathy whisper called to him from the woods. "Zach," it said.

Zach jerked his head back toward the voice. "Who's out there?"

No response.

"Is someone there?" he asked again.

A long moment of silence. Then the voice spoke again. "Michael." A little louder now. A little clearer.

"Michael? Tristan? Are you guys out there?" Zach trod closer to the sound of the mysterious voice. Twigs snapped under his feet as he ventured off the path. Branches surrounded him. He stuck his hands out to protect himself from the sharp limbs of the forest.

He was a few feet off the trail.

"Zach!" The voice again. Much louder now. A call for help.

"Michael, is that you? Where are you guys?"

No response. The snow was coming down harder now, blanketing the pine tree's branches. Zach's cotton hat and jacket were smothered in flakes. He shivered in the cold. His spring jacket was too light and he had brought no gloves. He couldn't see them in the dark, but he imagined his fingertips were blue. He jammed them into his pockets. His right hand slammed into Chris's stone. Almost immediately his fingers felt relief. Warmth radiated from the surface of the stone. After taking the stone out of his pocket, Zach cupped it with both hands, allowing the blood to flow through his fingers again.

He didn't understand it. How could a rock be doing this? But he was in no position to worry about it. Maybe there was a scientific reason for it. Maybe some rocks give off heat.

"Tristan." The voice spoke again. It was near.

Zach had to find out who or what it was.

With the rock safely in his pocket and new warmth flowing through him, Zach strode deeper into the woods. The only respite from the blackness of the forest was the heavy, white snowfall.

Zach continued. Step after step, blocking the branches with his forearms. The minutes passed. "That voice couldn't have been this far away. Michael! Tristan!" he yelled.

The voice had vanished.

Zach looked around. Trees. Snowfall. Darkness. The clearing of the path was gone. He didn't know how to get back to the trail. If he was lost before, then he was really lost now.

Then it came. The smell. Gasoline. Burnt rubber. It came as if it was oozing from the surrounding tree branches. It overwhelmed Zach and he gagged. He kept moving through the forest as quickly as he could, trying to escape the odor, but it followed him relentlessly.

He was deep into the forest. Michael and Tristan were nowhere to be found. The cold air snapped the air from his lungs. The forest seemed to be caving in on him from every direction.

It was clear now. Whatever was out there haunting him had also tricked him. Michael and Tristan had never been here. But something else was, and for Zach there was no escape.

Chapter 12

Logan

LOGAN KNOCKED FRANTICALLY on Mr. Foster and Mr. Loeb's door. No answer. It was 2:00 in the morning. They had to be in there. "Mr. Foster? Mr. Loeb?"

Still no answer.

He gave up knocking and turned back toward his own room. The two teachers stood before him looking concerned. "What's up, Logan?" asked Mr. Foster.

"Oh, I am glad you're here. I tried knocking on your door and you didn't answer. I wasn't sure what to do. I didn't know where to find you."

"Slow down," said Mr. Loeb. "It's okay. We were waiting in the lobby in case Michael and Tristan showed up. What can we do for you?"

"Michael and Tristan haven't been found yet?"

"Afraid not," said Mr. Loeb. "But there are a lot of people out looking. They'll turn up soon, I'm sure."

"Well, I wasn't sleeping very well. Tossing and turning all night. So, finally I just got up to get my book, so I could do a little reading. I thought I would see if Zach was awake, but when I looked up at his bed, he wasn't there. So now all three of my roommates are gone."

"Do you have any idea where he might have gone?" asked Mr. Foster.

Logan thought for a moment. What had Zach said to him? "They aren't going to find them." Zach had sounded certain of it, like he was the only one who could solve this mystery.

Logan looked at Mr. Foster and Mr. Loeb. "I don't know for sure, but I would bet he went to find Michael and Tristan."

Mr. Foster and Mr. Loeb looked at each other. "Does he know something about what happened to them?" asked Mr. Foster.

Logan was silent.

"Logan?" Mr. Loeb prompted.

Logan had never lied to an adult in his life. He turned to look at Mr. Foster. "Not that I know of," he said. "Maybe he just wanted to help." They wouldn't believe Zach's ghost story anyway. He wasn't even sure if he believed it, but something was clearly bothering Zach. Whether it was a ghost or not, Logan wasn't sure.

"Okay, well, we'd better go tell Mrs. Lomeier about this," said Mr. Loeb. "They need to know that they're looking for three kids now instead of two. Logan, you stay here. Mr. Foster and I will be right back. Logan, would you mind waiting here in the lobby in case any of them show up?"

Logan nodded.

After the two teachers had left, Logan sat on the couch in the lobby, leaning over with his elbows on his knees. "They aren't going to find them," Zach had said. Maybe Zach was right. Maybe the teachers and staff at Pine Ridge didn't know what they were dealing with. Maybe they had no idea how to find Michael and Tristan. And maybe they had no idea how to find Zach either.

Logan couldn't sit around and wait for nothing to happen. He had to do something.

Logan barged into his room and put on his warm clothes. His winter coat. His long underwear. His stocking hat and gloves. Inside, he had already begun to sweat, but he knew that he would need them once he got outside. He had to hurry before Mr. Foster and Mr. Loeb returned. In the side pocket of his backpack was a water bottle. It was empty. So on his way out he stopped at the drinking fountain and filled it. Then he placed it in the pocket of his coat.

The lobby was empty. He could get out undetected.

Logan stepped outside on to the white path. The falling snow had covered much of it. It must have dropped fifteen degrees since the last time he had been outside. Without the campfire and flashlights, the campus seemed eerily isolated, as if it had suddenly been transplanted into an episode of *The Twilight Zone*.

He glanced around, wondering which way Zach might have gone. He had no idea. Melanie had said there were eighteen miles of trails in the area. How would he ever find the right one? He didn't know, so he picked a trail and headed in that direction.

As he walked toward the closest trail directly behind the campfire pit, a faint glow caught his eye. A light in the window of the girls' dorm. He turned and crept toward the light to get a closer look. Snowflakes brushed his eyelashes. He wiped them off with his glove, and then peered toward the light again.

It was Jenny's room.

She sat on her bed reading a book, a small reading light illuminating the pages. Logan took off his hat. He didn't want to creep her out when he went to the window. He tapped lightly on the glass. She looked up. When she saw Logan, she smiled, like she had expected him to come.

Logan waved to her and pointed toward the front door.

Jenny nodded.

Logan then moved around toward the front, waiting for her to come out. He could see into the lobby. There were no teachers waiting. There was no one there to stop her. She would be able to escape easily, just as he had.

Logan waited for a few minutes. What was keeping her? Finally, Jenny calmly wandered out the front door dressed in a thick ski jacket, snow pants, mittens and a hat. She looked adorable, all bundled up from head to toe.

"What are you doing up this late?" Logan asked.

"I couldn't sleep. I kept thinking about Michael and Tristan."

"Your roommates didn't seem to have a problem with it," Logan joked.

"Yeah, they could sleep through anything. Why are you out here at 2:30 in the morning?"

Logan looked out to the trees, then turned back to face Jenny. "Zach is missing now too."

Jenny's jaw dropped.

"I think he went to search for Michael and Tristan. He thinks he can find them."

"Why does he think that? There are people all around here that know this area a lot better than him." Jenny paused for a moment, thinking. "Wait. Does this have anything to do with that 'disappearing truck' thing?"

"I'm not sure." Logan didn't want to reveal the fact that Zach believed he was being haunted. He didn't want to tell Jenny that Zach believed Michael and Tristan's disappearance was related to a ghost that had been haunting Pine Ridge. That story could wait.

"So, you haven't told me what you're doing out here yet," Jenny said.

"I'm going after Zach. I need to find him."

"How are you going to do that? It's the middle of the night. It's snowing. It's freezing. You don't even know where he went. You should wait for the adults to find him. They know what they're doing. See, look over there." Jenny pointed toward the administrative building. There were lights on inside. Mrs. Lomeier, Mr. Foster, Mr. Loeb and Miss Pliska were talking inside with a man in uniform. A police car was parked in the lot next door.

"The police are here?" Logan said. "They must really have no idea where they are. Maybe Zach does know something. Maybe he is their only chance. But what if Zach's in trouble? It's freezing out there. I have to try to do something to help him. If the teachers and police can't find Michael and Tristan, there is no reason for me to think they can find Zach either."

"You at least need to tell them that Zach is missing," Jenny pleaded.

"I told Mr. Foster and Mr. Loeb already. That's why they're over there. They're probably talking to Lomeier and the police about him right now." Logan gazed into the lighted window, watching the adults as he spoke. "I'd better go before they come out and see us here," he said.

Jenny gave no response.

Logan faced the dark, mysterious forest and made his way toward the path. Before he made it to the campfire pit he stopped. Light footsteps crunched the snow-topped gravel close behind him. He spun around.

Jenny stood in front of him. She looked up at Logan with honest, convincing eyes and said, "I'm going with you."

Chapter 13

Zach

THE VOICES THAT HAD summoned Zach had gone quiet. He wandered for a while, trying to find his way back to the path, but with no luck.

He had lost all sense of time. He knew he had left around midnight, but he had no clue how long he had been out in the woods. In his rush to get out of the dorm, he had left his phone in the room. He wasn't sure it would even get a signal out here anyway. The only thing he was sure of was that he was exhausted and he needed to rest.

The snow was making it even more difficult to find his way through the forest. It made it hard to spot fallen branches and rocks. Zach kept tripping over them, causing him to fall. The journey was a workout, harder than any baseball or basketball practice.

As he continued to trudge through the thick brush, pushing branches out of his way to avoid getting hit in the face, he came upon a fallen tree. Its trunk created a bridge above the ground as it rested against the massive trunk of a Black Spruce. Underneath the fallen tree, the ground was black, not white. Shelter from the snowfall.

"I need to rest," Zach said under his breath, careful not to speak too loudly. He didn't want to wake any ghosts or mysterious voices.

Zach found a spot where the fallen shaft was braced by the pine tree. He ducked under the trunk, gingerly sat on the damp, cold ground, and then leaned back against the pine tree. The rough bark scraped against his back, but he didn't care. The stiffness in his calves and quads relaxed immediately.

Zach leaned his head back and rested. He closed his eyes and within minutes was fast asleep.

Zach wandered down the middle of the street. Skyscrapers towered on either side of the road, hiding the sky above.

He was alone.

A traffic light flashed red on the next block. When he reached the next street, he turned right. In the middle of the otherwise empty boulevard was a water fountain. It spouted its liquid straight into the air. The peak of the water nearly reached the top of the tallest skyscraper.

"How is that even possible?" Zach wondered aloud.

He moved closer to the fountain expecting to be pelted by the falling water. But no water fell to the ground. It was as if it vaporized into the air.

Zach studied the phenomenon, not taking his eyes off the water's peak. Then he heard a faint voice on the other side of the fountain. "Zach."

Zach stepped to the side of the spout to take a closer look. Someone was standing on the far side of the fountain toward the end of the block.

He couldn't make out who it was. The voice spoke again. "Zach, let's play."

The fountain was behind him now. He began to walk toward the figure, which was coming toward Zach as well.

As they inched closer to each other, the face became clear. Zach stopped. The nameless character also paused.

It was a boy. He looked a bit younger than Zach. He wore jeans and a plain blue t-shirt. His hair was a bit messy and thick, round glasses circled his eyes.

"Chris?" Zach called. "Chris, is that you?"

"Yeah, it's me. Let's go play in the water fountain. Come on."

Chris walked past Zach, beckoning him to follow.

"You're alive. I can't believe you're alive! Where have you been, Chris? What happened to you that day in Duluth?"

"Don't worry, Zach. Come on. Let's play."

Zach followed Chris to the fountain.

As they approached the colossal spray, small drops of water began to plink on the pavement. It was no longer disappearing in the air. Zach looked up, but Chris continued toward the fountain. The drops of water were get-

ting bigger now. It was falling hundreds of stories to the ground. "Chris, wait!" Zach called.

"Come on, Zach. Let's play," Chris said.

"No, the water is going to fall on you! Come back!"

Zach ran towards Chris. He had to pull him away from the fountain. He had to save him.

He was almost there. He was within his reach. Zach reached his hand out to grab his brother and pull him out of the way, but before he could reach him, thousands of gallons of water dropped from the sky blocking Chris from Zach's view.

"No!" Zach yelled. He turned away from the gushing water and ran down the street.

A loud roar bellowed behind him. He turned around. A tidal wave rushed at him. He ran to one side, but the buildings blocked any path of escape. He turned toward the other side of the street. Still no way out. The water was too close now. He would never outrun it. He stopped in the middle of the street and faced the oncoming water.

Fifty feet away. Twenty feet. Ten.

Chapter 14

Logan

LOGAN AND JENNY HIKED down the path at a quick pace. They chose to take the same path they traveled for the night hike. Shortly after they had begun their search, Jenny had stuffed her hands into her coat pockets. "Hey, look what I brought," she said.

"What's that?"

Jenny pulled her iPhone from her pocket. "Check it out." She turned on her phone, touched the flashlight app, and immediately the glow of the screen lit the forest around them. She flashed the phone into the woods. Trees, branches, snowflakes, and the chasm of darkness suddenly became visible. "Now that we can see a little bit, it looks pretty creepy in there."

"Yeah, you're right," said Logan. "But it might come in handy if we need to see something in the dark."

"I haven't used this at all since we've been here. The battery is completely full."

The pair continued to walk at a brisk pace down the trail.

"Zach! Zach! You out here?" Logan called.

"Shush!" Jenny said. "Voices carry out here. They'll hear us back at camp if we're too loud."

Logan nodded and lowered his voice to a whisper. "Zach. Zach," he said.

There was no response. Only the chill of the wind and the soft crackle of snow under their feet as they walked. Logan pulled the water bottle from his coat pocket, popped the lid and took a swig. "You want some?" he asked Jenny.

Jenny took the bottle and drank. "We can't drink too much right now. We may need it later."

Logan nodded in agreement.

A moment of silence passed between them. Then Jenny spoke. "You never explained why Zach came out here by himself. Why did he think he could find Michael and Tristan without any help?"

Logan looked at Jenny. The light from her phone illuminated the freckles around her nose and her smooth, white teeth.

"If I tell you, you'll laugh."

"Try me."

"Okay. You asked for it," Logan said, a grin on his face. Logan told Jenny everything Zach had told him. The old truck Zach had seen. The strange smell. The haunting during KP duty. The strange figure in the woods. Miranda's story. "I haven't seen any of this stuff happen, but all I know is that I have never seen Zach act like this before. Since his brother went missing, he's been pretty unpredictable, but nothing like this. Something is really bugging him."

"You're telling me there is some ghost out here and it's after Zach?"

Logan shrugged. "Who knows? But Zach certainly thinks so and he seems determined to get to the bottom of it. We have to find him."

"Then let's find him."

The two hiked through the falling snow, careful not to leave the safety of the trail. They walked closely together. Logan could feel Jenny's shoulder brushing against his—he didn't move away. They followed the light of Jenny's phone until a rustling in the nearby woods suddenly interrupted the peace.

"What is that?" Logan asked.

"What? I didn't hear anything."

Just off to the right of the path, the snow crunched. Footsteps.

"Over there." Logan pointed toward the birch trees on the right hand side of the path.

Jenny shined her phone in the direction of Logan's finger. "I don't see anything."

"Just listen for a second."

The sound was different now. Quicker and lighter. No more crunching snow. It sounded like animal claws scratching the bark.

"I hear it now," Jenny said.

"Hand me the phone," Logan said. Logan took the phone from Jenny and slowly crept toward the edge of the trail.

A scrambling of footsteps again. Quicker still and higher above Logan and Jenny's heads. Logan pointed the phone toward the top of a tall, skinny birch.

"What is it?" asked Jenny.

"I don't know. I don't see anything." Logan peered into the tree, searching for the sound's source.

Jenny took a step away from the tree. "Come on, let's get out of here," she said.

"Wait. It might just be an animal or something."

"Do we really want to find out?"

Logan turned back toward the trail.

Suddenly, something scurried down the tree past Logan and Jenny. Jenny gasped as it appeared from Logan's backside.

A squirrel.

As the rodent crossed the trail, Jenny exhaled.

They both laughed.

"Let's keep going," said Logan.

Jenny walked on Logan's left side. They giggled, thinking of the "squirrel ghost" as Logan had called it.

Suddenly, Jenny stopped laughing and grabbed Logan's arm. "What's that?" she asked.

Logan jumped.

"Geez, you scared the crap out of me," Logan said light-heartedly. "Relax. It was just a squirrel. Let's keep going."

"No. Not the squirrel. What is that over there?" Jenny pointed back toward the forest.

Deep in the woods was a shape. A glowing figure.

Logan squinted to get a better look as he made his way off the trail. He couldn't make out any facial features. All he could see was a light, orangey glow outlining the shape.

Logan expected the forest to be bright, illuminated by the figure's radiance. But it wasn't. The glow was isolated to the mysterious shape. There were no shadows cast on the branches. The light seemed to defy physics. All the vegetation was still trapped in darkness.

Jenny stood by Logan's side. "What is it?" she asked. "Another animal?"

Logan lifted Jenny's phone to light the woods. He hoped to get a better look at the mysterious sight. As he shined the light toward the figure, it disappeared. "It's gone," he said.

Jenny looked up at Logan. "Could that have been . . . ?"

Before she could finish her sentence, Logan grabbed her hand and pulled her back toward the trail. "Let's keep going," he said.

"You want to stay out here? Shouldn't we head back to the camp? I'm scared, Logan."

As Logan opened his mouth to respond, the light on Jenny's phone vanished. "I thought you said the battery was full on this thing."

"It was. It was totally full when I turned it on."

Logan handed the phone to Jenny. She tried to turn it on again. Nothing. No power. No light. She shook it and then beat it on her palm. "This is weird."

Logan took his eyes off the phone and turned toward the dark forest. "Yeah . . . this is weird. I think you might be right. Let's head back toward camp. We can talk to the teachers and police and maybe they can help. Maybe they've already found them."

Logan and Jenny turned around. But Logan's feet were suddenly stuck. Stuck in a foot of snow. Jenny's feet were too. Their path was gone. They had somehow been transported away from the trail. They stood in the middle of the forest, surrounded by darkness.

"Oh my God! Where are we?" cried Jenny.

Logan looked around, trying to find his way back to the trail, but he found nothing but dense forest. The trail was gone. He turned back toward Jenny.

"Logan, look," she said, her voice quivering.

Directly in front of them, about ten feet away was the glowing figure. It had narrow, burning eyes. Its face was black, camouflaged by the surrounding darkness. Its legs seemed to disappear before they reached the ground, so it floated directly above the snow cover. Its arms stretched into the trees, blending into the branches. They seemed infinitely long.

Logan and Jenny were speechless, mesmerized by the specter in front of them. Then its ghostly arms emerged from the foliage of the pines. The handless appendages circled around Logan and Jenny, passing easily through the thick tree trunks. They formed a cage around the two.

Jenny screamed. "What do we do?" she called to Logan.

"Run!" Logan said.

But they couldn't move. Their feet were stuck in the snow. Some force was weighing them down. They struggled for a moment as the arms closed around them.

Jenny's face was full of terror. Her mouth was open and her eyes were wide, looking to Logan for safety. "What do we do?" she asked.

Logan stared deeply into the fiery eyes of the creature. This was the ghost that had been haunting Zach. Everything about his story had been true. Now this thing, this specter, was after him and Jenny.

Logan grabbed Jenny's hand and held it in his own. With a stoic, emotionless voice, he said, "We're trapped."

Chapter 15

Zach

ZACH WOKE IN A COLD SWEAT. The vision of his brother being swallowed by the gush of falling water had been nightmarish. Here he was, lost in the woods in complete darkness, being haunted by a ghostly specter, exhausted and hungry, and the thing that disturbed him the most was a dream about his missing brother.

He didn't know how long he had been asleep. The snow was still falling, but it was lighter now. The flakes were not as large and they seemed to be reaching the ground much more slowly than before.

He had been bitten by the cold. His hands, his toes, and every one of his muscles were chilled. Zach knew he needed to get up and start moving again, but his body wouldn't let him.

He stared off into the dark forest, clasping his arms around his chest, trying to create heat from a body that seemed to be completely devoid of warmth. He sat, shivering.

Eventually, his lower back began to ache. He was no longer leaning against the tree. He was sitting straight up, "Indian style." But he could not hold the position any longer, so he moved away from his tree shelter and stood.

He shoved his hands into his coat pockets. The rock. He pulled it out, hoping it would create the warmth it had earlier that night.

Zach held the stone with both of his fists clenched together.

Nothing.

He gripped the stone harder.

Still . . . nothing.

Finally, he lifted his two fists, the rock firmly between them, high above his head. He closed his eyes tightly, trying to pull the heat from the rock with his own intensity.

Suddenly, a tingling crawled through his hands and into his forearms. It traveled to his shoulders, through his neck, and then down to his chest. His shivering calmed. The warmth continued to his legs, feet, and toes. It was as if someone had flipped a switch on his internal thermostat.

Relieved, Zach lowered the rock, opened his hands and studied it. It was difficult to see in the darkness. It wasn't glowing. The gritty, sharp feel of it had not changed. There did not seem to be anything magical about the stone. Was this all in his head? Was this ordinary rock really responsible for keeping him warm? Maybe even for keeping him alive?

Zach took another step away from the tree. He had new energy. New life. Michael and Tristan were still out there somewhere and he had to find them.

Zach trudged his way through the snow and the dense forest. He felt a painful, burning sensation on his left cheek, just under his eye. Sharp twigs and branches had been pelting his body as he walked. A branch must have slapped him in his face. Was he bleeding? Would he need stitches? His hands were much warmer now, but they ached from having to grab so many sharp branches. There were cuts and splinters all over his fingers and palms. More than ever he wished he had brought his gloves.

After fifteen minutes of aimless hiking, Zach came to a clearing. A small reprieve from the torture of the dagger branches. It was a circle that two fallen birch trees had created amid the dense forest.

Zach stood up straight. Having to hunch over as he walked, ducking and dodging obstacles, it felt nice to straighten his already sore back. He touched the cut on his cheek softly with his fingers. It was moist. Blood.

He put his hands together to relieve the pain from the cuts. Then he held them out in front of his body, his palms toward the sky. Light snowflakes fell on his cuts relieving the pain slightly.

Zach took a deep breath and began walking out of the clearing and back into the trees. He reached out his hand to move the first branch out of the way. But before he grabbed the prickly pine, he stopped. He squinted his eyes. He turned around and moved back to the middle of the clearing. If the rock had warmed him, could it also help heal his wounds?

He took the stone out of his pocket and began with the cut on his cheek. Raising the rock to his face, he gently placed it on the bleeding wound. It stung instantly and Zach jerked the stone away from his face. The stone was gritty. It had sand particles on its surface, which caused the pain. He touched his cut with his fingers. It still hurt. It was still bleeding. He had to give it another try.

Once again, he moved the rock toward his face and placed it on the cut. He winced in pain, but he held it there longer this time. He counted to thirty in his head, speeding the numbers up the longer he held the stone to his face. Twenty-eight . . . twenty-nine . . . thirty! He took the stone from his still stinging cheek. Then he touched the cut again with his fingers. No change. He was certain it was still bleeding.

Zach decided to try the rock's powers on the cuts on his hands. He grabbed the stone with his left hand and gently rubbed the cuts on his right hand. No relief. Just more painful stinging. He tried again on the cuts of his left hand. Same result. Why wasn't it working? Why will it warm me, but not heal my cuts?

Zach pocketed the stone and continued on through the woods, stopping to rest more frequently now. He panted in the cold air. One hour passed. Then two.

The cuts on his hands no longer bothered him. They had become numb. It wasn't the rock's doing. He had become immune to the pain the way a boxer might after being punched hundreds of times in one bout.

The snow had ceased. Only a few stray flakes continued to fall. Zach was relieved. If the snow had gotten much deeper he wasn't sure if he would have been able to continue. Without snow boots hiking was difficult enough.

He had no idea where he was headed. He just hoped he would find something soon. A trail. A building. A hat or glove. Maybe even Michael and Tristan.

Zach stopped to take a break. He moved out of the way of a thick evergreen branch and stood up straight. He closed his eyes and breathed deeply, remembering how effective that could be when he was on the pitcher's mound. It calmed him. Relaxed him. It took him away from peril and into a lonely, but peaceful place.

When he opened his eyes a glorious sight loomed in the distance. Through the triangular shapes of trees, the morning sky had appeared. The clouds dispersed allowing the sunrise to light the day. It was faint, but the mixture of vermillion and orange was unmistakable.

Zach had never felt relief like this before. He squinted his eyes to make sure they had not been mistaken. In the distance, there it was. The sun was rising.

Chapter 16

Logan

LOGAN OPENED HIS EYES. He was no longer in the thick, dark forest. He was inside, sitting at a kitchen table, staring out the window. The lights were bright inside. Outside a hint of daylight started to peak through the fading clouds.

He looked around the kitchen. It was small, like the one in his parents' cabin on Big Sandy Lake. On the opposite side of the room was a white General Electric refrigerator. It was old and had a silver handle that could be pulled out from the door. One of Logan's neighbors had disposed of a refrigerator just like it in their back alley.

The sink was to the right of the refrigerator, with three cupboards overhead. Below Logan's feet was a musty, worn out carpet.

He blinked his eyes three times, trying to regain his wits. The last thing he remembered was being circled by a ghostly figure in the middle of the forest. Jenny was beside him then.

He looked around the kitchen again. He was alone. Where had Jenny gone? Where had she been taken?

Logan stood up quickly, knocking his chair over. He had no idea where he was. He had no idea who or what had brought him here. But he knew he had to find Jenny and get back to Pine Ridge.

A wooden swinging door closed the kitchen off from the rest of the house. Logan made his way to the exit. He put his hand on the door and eased it open slowly. On the other side of the door was a small, square-shaped living room. The furnishings consisted of two kitchen chairs and a small end table pushed up against the wall. It looked as if someone had come in and stolen all of the furniture from the home.

On the table was a small lamp. It emitted a dim light, which, combined with dawn's sunlight, created an eerie, shadowy tone within the room. Directly under the lamp was a bowl of rocks. They were all different sizes, colors, and shapes and looked to be hand picked. A collection maybe.

There was no carpet in the room. Just an old stained hardwood floor. On the wall was a crooked painting of an older man with two younger men sitting in chairs below him. The two younger individuals looked like the man's sons, but Logan couldn't be sure of that.

He stepped further into the living room. He was still alone. No dark specter. No Jenny.

A door was opened a crack on the far side of the room. After a closer look, Logan realized that it was a bathroom.

Logan wasn't sure where else to look. The home was small and, as far as he knew, he had seen it all. "Jenny?" he spoke softly, hoping she was nearby. When there was no response, he called again a bit louder this time. "Jenny? Are you here?"

Silence.

Another door was framed on the far wall. "That must lead outside," Logan whispered to himself.

He moved toward the door. As he reached out his hand to pull the handle, he heard the faint cry of a girl's voice.

"Logan."

It had to be Jenny. She was calling from outside.

He grabbed the handle of the door, but pulled his hand away. It was hot. Scorching hot. He held his hand under his left armpit to ease the pain. Then he pulled the sleeve of his coat over his left hand and tried opening the door again. No luck. It seemed to be even hotter now.

Even though he could move about the cabin freely, he was being held prisoner. How would he get out? He needed to help Jenny. She could be in trouble.

He paced along the side of the home, close to the outer wall. Heat resonated along the perimeter. He leaned in closer. It felt as if the wall was on fire. The entire building was laced with intense heat. There was no way out.

Logan backed away from the wall, moving toward the center of the living room. He no longer heard Jenny's voice. What could he do to escape? Although his gloves were in his coat pockets, his palms were still sweaty with fear.

Logan paced back and forth, the floor creaking with every step. He realized that although the walls were too hot to touch, the floor was not. He spun around and moved back toward the front door. As he approached the door, the sound of the hardwood below him suddenly changed from a low, steady creaking, to a high-pitched squeak.

Logan looked down. His right foot stood in the center of four grooves that formed a perfect square. Bending to floor level, he reached out his hand to feel the shape below him, and then he stopped. Logan grabbed his gloves from his coat pocket and slid one on his right hand. With his gloved hand, he reached down and carefully touched his fingertips to the floor. He had to be sure he wouldn't get burnt again.

The floor wasn't hot, at least not with his glove on. Logan took off the glove and then touched the wood square again. It didn't burn his hand.

"There has to be a way out of here," Logan said.

He pushed on the floorboards, hoping the square was a trap door. It didn't budge. He pushed harder and harder, exerting all of his energy. It was no use. The square wouldn't move.

Logan sat back, breathing hard. He scanned the cabin. Then shouted, "Let me out of here! Whoever you are, let me out of here!"

Nothing. "Okay. Calm down Logan. There has to be a way out of this place. There is always a solution to every problem. Solve the problem. Solve the problem." He looked down. Below his feet a light shined. A small glimmer found its way through the grooves in the wooden square. The floor had moved after all.

Logan put both of his gloves on to protect his hands from the pressure of the floorboards. With renewed hope, he pushed on the square again. He could feel it creeping downward. The light became brighter and brighter with each shove of Logan's hands.

Logan took another break. His arms were tired and his hands, despite the protection of his gloves, were sore. He pulled the water bottle from his coat pocket and took a drink. The cool, wet liquid felt good on his dry throat.

After putting the bottle back in his pocket, Logan took a deep breath, gathered all his strength, and with both hands shoved the floorboards down as hard as he could. The floor snapped opened and Logan grabbed the edges of the grooves to keep himself from falling through. Below the floor was dirt with a few scattered patches of snow. It was morning now, but shadows kept the ground dark. "Where does this go?"

Logan peeked his head through the hole in the floor. Looking left, he saw the underside of a rickety porch extending just beyond the door above.

He pulled his head back into the home. "Why is this trap door here? Why would there be a way out when I'm trapped here in every other way? It doesn't make sense." But he had no choice. He had to get out and going through the floor was his only chance.

He braced himself with his hands on either side of the trap door. Gravity pushed him through the opening, but he was able to use his strength to slowly lower himself to the ground.

When his feet touched the dirt below, he got to his hands and knees to crawl underneath the porch. A lattice barrier surrounded the bottom perimeter of the porch. Directly ahead of him were the stairs leading from the front door. How am I going to get out of here without breaking through the wood?

Logan inched his way forward, careful not to sit up too high. When he got to the edge of the porch, he looked through the holes of the lattice. A large clearing was directly in front of him. The front yard had been cleared of trees. *Jenny is out there somewhere*, he thought. He grabbed the lattice and shook it, trying to pry it loose. It was solidly intact.

Logan scooted around to face the outer edges of the barrier. He crawled along the edge of the porch looking for an escape. When he reached the corner, he turned to the left and stopped. In the very back corner was a cracked piece of lattice. Logan scurried to it, feeling the hard, rough ground scrape his knees.

Grabbing the broken wood with both hands, he pulled with all his strength. The wood snapped in two, leaving a small opening in the lattice. "I still can't fit through this."

He shook the other pieces of wood and found that they were loose. Laying on his back and pressing both feet to the weakened lattice, he pushed. Two other pieces of wood snapped. "This might be big enough now."

Logan stuck his head through the opening first. Then he flipped himself over on his back to pull the rest of his body through. He grimaced as the shattered pieces of wood scraped along his body. When his legs and feet cleared the hole, he collapsed on the ground.

Logan looked toward the cabin. From the front, the home looked small, just as it had when he was inside. The porch was wide and had a wooden railing wrapped around it. Two brown wicker chairs sat on the floor of the veranda. The roof of the cabin was made of birch bark and it angled slightly downward over the porch.

He stood, looking at all sides of the building. Extending out from the kitchen was an addition made of thick logs. It was as large as the original home. The color of the wood was slightly less worn, making it clear that it was not part of the original structure. *There must have been another exit out of the kitchen*, Logan thought. How did I miss it? And If someone really wanted to keep me prisoner here, why was I able to go through the floor? Why wasn't that hot too? What am I missing?

The only thing he knew was that he was free and he had to find Jenny.

He ran to the clearing in front of the house, looking all around him. Then he turned back, wanting to circle to the back of the cabin. Before he reached the trees, he stopped. A burning sensation overcame him. The kind of burning you feel after standing next to a blazing fire for an hour.

Logan had only been standing there a few seconds when directly in front of him violent flames appeared, towering over him. He backed up quickly, retreating toward the middle of the clearing. Logan turned to his left, hoping to find another escape route, but the flames were everywhere. The entire front yard of the cabin was surrounded by fire. It formed a circle, trapping Logan in the middle. They seemed to be taunting him, laughing at him.

Now Logan understood why he was able to leave the house. There was no easy escape after all.

Chapter 17

Zach

DAWN GAVE ZACH NEW LIFE. New hope to find his way home. New hope to find Michael and Tristan.

The snow no longer fell and the newly birthed sunlight poked through the tree branches, allowing Zach to make his way through the forest more easily and quickly. "Thank God I can see where I'm going," Zach said. His cuts still stung, but the hope of finding his way out of the tree maze dampened the pain.

The sun peered over the tips of the tall trees now. Stopping to rest, Zach sat down on a log. He took two long, deep breaths. He could not keep running in circles the way he had been. "Think, Zach. The sun is up now. I should be able to figure this out. Which way did I come from? Which direction is the dorm?" He spoke loudly as if he were talking to someone.

Zach looked through the trees to the sun. "Rises in the east, sets in the west," he said, remembering the saying he learned in third grade.

Mrs. Lomeier had shown his class a map of Pine Ridge back at school. Lake Superior lay directly to the east of the camp. "We walked directly toward the lake on the night hike," Zach said, much quieter this time. "So, the dorms must be the opposite direction."

Zach turned his back to the steadily rising sun and began walking to the west. He walked for a few minutes, dodging tree branches and stepping over logs and stones. But as he continued, the branches became lighter and less of an obstacle. He was able to walk upright now. The pain in his lower back was tempered.

Zach stopped walking and smiled. He now understood why the foliage had become lighter. A trail. First the sunrise and now this.

He took a few steps into the clearing and turned back toward the sunrise. Then back to the west. There was still no sign of Michael and

Tristan and he wasn't even sure where *he* was. But he had found his way back to a path. He would be able to find his way back to Pine Ridge now.

Zach jogged in the direction of the camp. Maybe Michael and Tristan were already back there. Maybe he was the only one missing now. He had done what he could to find them, but he did not want to risk getting lost again. If he did, he may never find his way out.

The snow made the running difficult. His feet sunk into the top layer with each step. He was exhausted, but he knew he could make it back if he just kept going.

Zach ran for ten minutes. Then he slowed to a walk. A steep hill rose in front of him. He would have to walk up a difficult incline.

He pulled the stone from his pocket and gripped it in his hand. He hoped it would give him the strength he needed to continue.

As he took his first step toward the hill, a voice echoed through the trees. "Zach!"

Zach whipped his head around. It had come from the east. Is it the ghost? Is it Michael or Tristan?

He turned his whole body around.

"Zach!"

The voice sounded familiar.

A figure appeared around the bend of the trail. He was tall and wearing a backpack. Zach inched toward him.

"Zach! Is that you?"

A man's voice. Zach stared in disbelief. "It can't be."

The man got closer and closer to Zach. He wore a stocking hat and he had a wide, sloped nose. His mouth was open and he was breathing heavily. He was big and strong.

"Oh my God," said Zach. "Dad?"

ZACH STOOD, LOOKING UP at his father. He wasn't sure what to do or say. Is this really my dad, or is it Victor Leppla playing some kind of sick trick on me? Miranda said he had mysterious powers.

"Zach, I can't believe I found you. Are you okay?"

Zach was silent. He stared curiously at his dad's face.

"Zach, it's okay. I'm here now. It's gonna be okay."

It sounded like his dad. It looked like his dad. But it didn't make any sense. Why was he here? How did he find me?

Robert Sutton held out his arms. His broad shoulders beckoned his son to come closer. Cautiously, Zach moved toward him. He laid his head on his chest, nestling into the comfort of his body. This felt like his dad.

He stayed in his father's arms for a few moments, silent and comfortable. Finally, Zach spoke. "What are you doing here? How did you find me?"

"Just relax," he said. "I'll explain everything soon. I just need to make sure you're okay first." He carefully pushed Zach away from him and looked into his eyes. "Are you sure you're okay?"

"I'm fine, Dad. Just really tired and hungry. And now I'm really confused."

"Yeah, I know you are," his dad said, rifling through his backpack. "Here, eat this." He handed Zach a protein bar. "I promise I'll clear everything up. But I think we should make our way back to campus first. Get you some more food and take care of these nasty cuts you've got. Whadda you say?"

Zach nodded, scarfing down the snack. "Do you know how to get back? I've been trying all night."

"You were headed in the right direction. You've always been a great problem solver, Zach. I know you would have found your way back whether I had shown up or not."

Zach and his dad walked toward the hill in front of them. The muscles in Zach's shoulders and neck relaxed with his father's strong arm around him.

As they began their assent up the hill, a bonfire-like crackling, paralyzed them.

Zach turned around to locate the sound. "What is that?" he asked.

His dad was silent.

Looking up at his father this time, he repeated, "Dad, what is that?"

Finally, Mr. Sutton turned in the direction of the sound, but still did not answer.

Zach scanned the forest. An orangey glow flickered through the trees. Flames. "Is that a . . . ? Dad, I think there's a fire out there! We'd better tell someone!"

Mr. Sutton grabbed Zach's arm. "Just wait, Zach."

"Wait? Someone has to put out that fire or the forest will burn!"

"Look," Robert said as he pointed toward the trees.

Zach followed his dad's hand with his eyes. "It's gone," he said. "How did it just stop like that? What's going on?"

"Zach, I think it's time we had a talk. And we should probably do it right now."

"Are we in danger, Dad?" Did his dad know something about Victor Leppla's ghost?

Robert led Zach to a fallen tree just off the path. He sat down. "Have a seat," he said, patting the log with his palm. "I've got something I need to tell you."

Chapter 18

Logan

LOGAN'S CAPTOR WAS TAUNTING him with the cage of fire. Red-hot flames would die down to mere candle flickers, giving Logan hope for an escape. But time after time, when Logan would make a run for it, the flames would swell again as he reached the perimeter.

He sat down in the middle of the clearing, tired of losing the unwinnable battle.

"Logan! Are you out there?" Jenny's voice echoed through the trees. It *had* been Jenny he heard when he was inside the house.

"Jenny, where are you?" he called back.

"We're behind the house by the creek!" This was a different voice. A boy's voice.

"Michael? Is that you?"

"Yeah! Tristan is here too!"

"Is everyone okay?"

Jenny spoke again. "Yeah, we're fine, but we can't leave this area. There is some kind of invisible barrier surrounding us. Where are you?"

"I'm in the front of the cabin. There's a fire blocking my way out."

"A fire?" Jenny called back.

Logan explained the fire's insolence. How it seemed to know when he was trying to escape. How it did just enough to torment him without burning him.

"How are we gonna get outta here, Logan?" asked Tristan.

"I don't know for sure, but we'll figure something out. We have to keep talking to each other so we know we're all right."

Logan scanned the area again, trying to find an escape that he might have missed before. Then he remembered something Michael had said. They were behind the house *by the creek*. Where did the creek go? Did it flow to the front of the house where he was trapped?

"Michael!" called Logan.

"Yeah, I'm here."

"Did you say there was a creek back there?"

"Yeah. It's right outside of this invisible wall we're trapped behind."

"Can you see if there is water flowing in it, or is it iced over?"

"There is still some water flowing." Jenny answered this time. "Why does that matter?"

"Umm, I'll get back to you in a minute," said Logan.

Logan walked to the edge of the clearing, the miniscule flames a few feet in front of him. Beyond the ring of fire, past the first line of birch trees, about fifteen yards from where he stood, ran a sloped ditch. He followed the ditch with his eyes. It ran toward the back of the house. *That has to be the creek,* he thought.

He backed up to the middle of the yard, placing himself in the center of the fire ring, the remaining snow crunching under his feet. He bent over, placing his hands on his knees. Inhaling a mixture of smoke and cool, fresh air, he stood tall again. "This is the only way out," he reminded himself.

Logan felt the air fill up his lungs. Then he opened his eyes wide and ran as fast as he could. He was never as fast as Zach, but he could hold his own. He ran straight for the fire. And he was not going to stop.

It took only seconds, but it felt like a lifetime. When he reached the flames, they erupted high over his head as expected. But Logan kept running right through the scorching fire. As he passed through the flames, he ducked his head and closed his eyes tightly.

When he emerged he felt pain. His coat and pants were on fire. He could feel the sweltering heat burning through his clothes and on to his skin. He dropped to the ground and rolled, trying to extinguish the flames, but they were burning too fiercely. So he sprinted as fast as he could to the ditch, shedding his coat as he ran.

Logan slid down the slope of the ditch, his pants still burning. He submerged his body into the water. "Ahh!" he moaned in relief.

After the flames were extinguished and his body had cooled, Logan surfaced from the water and struggled out of the ditch.

The burning sensation turned icy-cold. The cool air chilled Logan to his core. His clothes were wet and his coat had burned to near ashes.

Logan sat on the snowy ground, his arms wrapped around his chest, shivering. His legs hurt. They had been burned the worst. His upper body had been somewhat protected by his thick winter coat that he had ripped off his body.

He looked to the front yard where the fire had been. No flames. No heat to warm him.

Logan struggled to his feet, his arms still cradling his body. He walked slowly along the side of the house, where he could clearly see the addition on the back of the building. He passed the kitchen window. Then a den. An upright piano stood in the corner. At the end of the addition was a dark room. It was a small chamber, about the same size as the kitchen. The natural light shined through the window. In the middle of the room was a table with a circle of rocks lying on top of it. Otherwise, the room was empty. Logan remembered the bowl of rocks in the living room of the cabin.

The pain shot through Logan's legs, causing him to hunch over. He walked toward the backyard with his left hand on the house, bracing him.

"Jenny?" Logan's voice trembled with the cold.

"We're here Logan!" said Jenny.

Logan reached the back edge of the house. Jenny, Michael, and Tristan stood next to a large pine tree.

"Look!" Tristan called to Jenny and Michael.

Jenny and Michael turned to see Logan walking toward them.

"How did you escape?" asked Michael.

Logan didn't respond. He kept walking. His lips were blue and his teeth chattered.

"Logan, are you okay?" Jenny asked. "Wait! Stop! The barrier is right in front of you. It burns if you run into it."

Logan kept walking. He had heard Jenny's warning, but the pain in his legs and the cold in his body was all he could think about.

He passed the barrier. It didn't burn. It didn't even stop him from joining his friends.

Jenny, Michael, and Tristan were speechless.

Logan walked a few more steps. At that moment he collapsed.

Jenny came running toward him. "Logan! What happened?" She got down on her knees and saw his blue lips and chattering teeth. "He's freezing," she said to Michael and Tristan, who were standing close behind her. She put her arms around him and rubbed her hands along his back, trying to keep him warm.

Tristan ran over to the perimeter of the backyard. He raised his hand and touched the invisible force field. A hot jolt ran through his hand. He quickly pulled it back and looked at Michael. "How did he get through the barrier?" he asked.

Before Michael had a chance to answer, Logan lifted his head. And with his shivering voice, he said, "You . . . can . . . come . . . in . . . but . . . you . . . can't . . . get . . . out."

Chapter 19

Zach

Zach SAT ON THE LOG, HIS DAD NEXT TO HIM. The sun had crept over the top of the trees now, brightening the shadows of the forest. "Dad, what's going on? Why are you here?"

"Son, what I'm about to tell you may be hard for you to believe."

"Try me," said Zach.

"Some of your friends are missing, right?"

Zach nodded. "My roommates, yeah."

"Your brother is missing too."

"Dad, I know Chris has been missing for over a year. What does that have to do with Michael and Tristan disappearing?"

"I think it may have everything to do with why your roommates are missing," said Robert.

"I'm so confused, Dad. Just tell me what's happening here!"

"Zach, after Chris's disappearance, I moved to Two Harbors."

"I know that." Zach was becoming impatient.

"If you will just let me speak, I'll explain everything," Robert said.

Zach didn't respond. He slid his hands under his thighs, feeling the rough bark scratch his palms. Then he waited for his dad's explanation.

"I moved to Two Harbors because I wanted to be close to this area. You see, Zach, I'm confident Chris is still out there somewhere. I truly believe he's alive and he may be a lot closer than you think."

"How close?" Zach asked.

His dad stood up, raised his arms, and looked out into the forest. "He could be right under our noses. I moved up here so that I could scour this forest for Chris. And that's what I've been doing for the past year."

"But why do you think he's in this forest?" Zach had so many questions. He hardly knew where to begin.

Robert sat down again. "That's the part you may have a hard time believing."

"I don't think that's possible after what I've been through the past two days."

"About eighty years ago, the most important industry around this area was logging. There were two large companies that dominated the business. One of the companies was run by a guy named Fredrik Sutinen and the other was run by—"

Zach interrupted. "Let me guess . . . Victor Leppla."

Zach's dad looked shocked. "How did you know that?" he asked.

"I met someone who knows about this story."

"Who is it?" Fear was in his father's voice.

"Her name is Miranda. She works in the cafeteria at Pine Ridge."

"What did she tell you about them?"

Zach rehashed Miranda's story. Fredrik becoming mayor of Finland. The rivalry between the two companies. The fire that caused Kristian Leppla's death. Victor's ghost. "Dad, Miranda's last name is Leppla. She's Victor Leppla's granddaughter."

Robert's face remained stoic. "Oh, my God," he said. "I can't believe I didn't know about her." He paused for a moment. "Do you believe everything she told you?"

Zach took a deep breath, stared across the trail into the brightening woods, and said, "Yeah, I think I do. If I would of heard her story a week ago, I probably would have laughed in her face. But now . . . it all makes sense."

"Why does it make sense?" Robert asked.

Zach looked his dad straight in the eye. "Because I think Victor Leppla is after me."

Mr. Sutton didn't look surprised.

Zach went on to explain the trauma he had been through since arriving at Pine Ridge. He told him about everything including the nauseating smell, "losing time" at the cafeteria, the missing truck, and the mysterious figure in the woods.

His dad nodded his head. "I was afraid of that," he said. "I guess I don't need to tell you that Miranda's story is true."

Zach jerked his head in his father's direction. He had not expected such a blunt response.

Robert continued. "But it sounds like she left out some important details. Details that you need to know." He looked into Zach's eyes. "Are you ready to hear the whole story? The whole story as it relates to *you*?"

"To me?" said Zach.

His father nodded.

"Yeah. I'd like to know what's going on out here," Zach said.

"Well, I suppose we should start with Fredrik Sutinen." Robert scooted along the log, trying to get more comfortable. "Zach, he was your great-great grandfather."

Zach showed no reaction to this bit of news. Nothing could surprise him anymore.

"He was an immigrant from Finland. When he and his family settled here, that's when they got into the logging business. Our family name became Sutton a generation later when immigration papers were misread by the government.

"Fredrik was very motivated and showed a lot of initiative. So, not only did he start a successful business with basically no money, but he also became the mayor of Finland, Minnesota. Pretty impressive, huh?"

"Yeah, it is, but what does this have to do with me and Chris?" Zach asked impatiently.

"It has everything to do with you, Zach. The feud between Fredrik and Victor was real. Victor's son was killed in a fire at the logging plant and Victor blamed Fredrik for it."

"Did Fredrik really cause the fire that killed Kristian?"

"Nobody knows," said Zach's dad. "There was never any proof, but Victor certainly thought so."

"So what did Victor do about it?" Zach was on the edge of the log waiting for the next chapter of the story. "Was he really some kind of witch? Miranda said her grandpa was a witch. Is that true?"

Robert paused for a moment. "What do you think?" he asked.

Zach nodded. "It makes sense, I guess. I've seen some crazy stuff up here. But I still don't understand what this has to do with me and Chris!"

"Be patient, Zach. I'm getting there. You see, Victor did have certain powers. And when his son was killed, he wanted revenge. So he laid a curse on the Sutinens. But it didn't stop there. The curse was to plague all the generations of the Sutinen family. And now the Sutton, family."

"That's where we come in, right?"

"Right. Our family is cursed, Zach."

Even with everything that had happened to Zach, those words were difficult to swallow. The idea that he was related to Fredrik Sutinen, that he was "cursed", seemed completely absurd, as if he were in some kind of horror movie. "So, what is the curse, exactly?"

"Think about it for a second. Do you remember me telling you about my younger brother?"

"Yeah, didn't he die in a car accident when he was little?"

"Yes. He was seven years old. And my dad's younger sister, your aunt, Beverly? Do you remember that story?"

Zach thought for a second. "Oh yeah! Didn't she die of some strange disease?"

"Tuberculosis. It was a very rare case. Almost no one gets tuberculosis anymore. She was only fourteen when it happened."

Zach could feel his dad looking at him. Waiting for him to put the puzzle together. "Dying of a rare disease. Killed in a car accident. Chris disappearing." Zach stood up and walked over to the trail. Then turned around to face his dad again. "They were all young. The curse must have something to do with Sutton *kids*, right? Something bad happens to them?"

"That's right. All of these tragic cases happened to a Sutton, or a Sutinen, who was under eighteen years old. There are other stories like that too, from earlier generations. But here's the thing, Zach. Apparently the curse doesn't hurt all of the Sutton kids. Nothing ever happened to my older brother, my uncle, or me. The list goes on."

Zach nodded. "Yeah, that's kind of weird. I wonder how Victor picks and chooses who gets hurt."

"Well," Robert continued. "Not only are the victims young, but they are the youngest. Every strange case I could find seemed to affect the *youngest* Sutton. But you could look at it another way too. Maybe this curse is meant to torture the survivors as well. The youngest members of a family being killed or disappeared? That takes its toll on everyone involved. It has certainly done that to our family. Maybe Victor realized he wouldn't have to attack all of the Suttons to make an impact on everyone. All the kids are cursed whether they're the ones hurt or not. You understand?"

Zach nodded. Everything his dad had said made sense. Everything except one thing. "Yeah, it's been torture for all of us, but I don't think he's done with me. Taking Chris, if that's really what happened, isn't enough. I'm not the youngest, but he still wants something from me. Why else would he be putting me through all of this? Why would he take my roommates? Why would he make me see all these weird things in the woods? The only other person I've met who has seen any of these things is Miranda and she's Victor's granddaughter! He haunts her because she wouldn't help him with the curse. Why is he haunting me?"

Robert stood next to the log as Zach paced back and forth on the trail. "Come here, Zach," he said, sitting down again. Zach went back to the log and sat next to his dad. Robert put his arm around Zach's shoulders, pulling him closer to him. "I wish I knew, Zach. Trust me, I wish I had all the answers, but I don't."

A couple of minutes passed as Zach considered everything that had been laid before him. He still had one more question. "Dad?"

"Yeah, buddy?"

Zach backed away and looked his dad in the eyes. "Why didn't you bring this up when Chris disappeared? Why did you keep it a secret?"

Robert didn't respond immediately. After gathering his thoughts, he finally answered Zach's question. "Son, for years, this legend has circulated throughout the Sutton family. My dad and grandpa used to joke about it at Christmas and Thanksgiving celebrations. No one really believed it. It was just a story they entertained us with. So, I never bought it either. Magic. Curses. Why *would* I believe it?"

Zach nodded in agreement.

"But when Chris went missing, I started to dig. I thought about my brother and my aunt. Then I found other Sutton kids who had died, disappeared, or come down with some terrible disease. Could all of this be coincidence? But what would your mother or the police have said if I had told them that Chris had been a victim of a family curse and the perpetrator had been dead for fifty years?"

"They would have laughed at you," said Zach.

"Exactly. So, as hard as it was to leave you after your mom and I divorced, I had to come up here so I could do some searching on my own. I started to read. The Internet, old letters and papers I rounded up at the college. Everything I read led me to the conclusion that Victor did want revenge for Kristian's death, whether Fredrik caused it or not. But there was one letter in particular that convinced me." Robert bent over, unzipped his backpack, and pulled out a folded piece of paper. It had yellow stains on it. It was old and worn. "Because Fredrik Sutinen was the mayor of Finland, many of his documents and letters had been archived, so I accessed them through the college library.

"Fredrik had saved a letter from Victor Leppla. I can't imagine what Fredrik must have felt while he read it. In the letter, Victor called him a murderer. He told him he and his family would pay for what he did. But it didn't end there. The whole letter was written in English except the final sentence, which was written in Finnish. I had to have it translated, but when I did, I was convinced the curse was for real."

"What did it say?" Zach asked.

Robert unfolded the piece of paper and pointed to the last line. SUOJELLA LAPSIA. "It says, 'Protect your children.'"

Zach looked at his father. He squinted his eyes, and said, "So, it's true."

"This is where Victor Leppla lived. After reading that letter I came here, to these woods. I've scoured this area looking for Chris, but I haven't had any luck."

"You haven't found any clues at all?"

"Well, there was one. A few months ago, in the middle of winter. The snow was deep and hard to walk through, but I was able to find something. An old cabin. Probably about a half-mile from where we are right now. It was weird. There was nobody there. All the doors were unlocked, as if someone wanted me to go in. So I did. At first, I couldn't find anything to help me find Chris, but then I did find a clue. On the table in the living room. A bowl of rocks."

"Chris had a rock collection!" Zach said.

"I know. After I found the collection, I searched every corner of the cabin, but couldn't find him or any sign of Victor until I stumbled onto a small, dark room at the back of the house. The only thing in the room was a table. On top of it were more rocks. They were in a circle like they were being used for some kind of game. Some kind of strange 'cursing game.'"

"So, what did you do then?"

"I went straight to the police. I didn't call you or your mom right away because I wanted to make sure the clue was legit."

"Did the police come look? What did they find?"

"When I returned to the area with the police, we couldn't find anything."

"You mean the rocks were gone?" Zach asked.

"No. The entire cabin was gone," Robert said. "It was as if it had vanished into thin air."

Zach sat quietly, soaking it all in. Then he remembered the old truck he saw in the woods. How it had been there, but then disappeared when he came back with his friends. "I think we should go look for the cabin together. I have a feeling it'll be there this time."

"Why do you say that?"

"I'm not sure. Just a hunch, I guess," said Zach.

"Well, if you think so, we should check it out. We may be able to find something to help us. Maybe even your friends. Maybe even Chris."

Zach and his dad got up from the log and made their way to the trail. "Dad?" Zach said.

Robert turned around to face his son.

"Why are you here now? Is it just a coincidence that you were here at the same time I was?"

"No. Actually, I got a phone call from your mom. Your teacher called her when you disappeared from the camp. So I came up to Pine Ridge and spoke to her. What's her name? Mrs. Lomeiner?"

"Lomeier," Zach corrected.

"Right. I told her I would start searching. The police were on their way, but I had a hunch I might find you out here."

Zach's dad put his arm around him. Your mom is on her way up here, too.

"Mom's coming here?" Zach asked.

"Yeah. She's pretty worried about you."

Zach turned away from his dad. He looked deeply into the forest. "How worried can she be? She doesn't even want me to live with her anymore."

"Is that what you think? Zach, your mom and I agreed that if your schoolwork and behavior didn't improve you would come and live with me because we felt it was time for you to make a change. But that was *my* idea. Your mom does not want you to leave. Trust me on that."

Zach gazed into the woods. As he turned around to face his dad, he nodded. "Maybe," he said.

Robert put his hand on Zach's shoulder.

Zach took two steps down the trail and turned around. "Dad," he said. "Victor's house is out there somewhere. Let's go find it."

Chapter 20

Logan

THE SUN WAS HIGHER now in the hazy, blue sky. The clouds, which had produced the overnight snow, had disappeared almost entirely. It was still chilly, but the weather was gradually warming.

Michael and Tristan walked diligently along the perimeter of the backyard, searching for some kind of breech in the barrier. Some way to escape. But they were having no luck. The barrier seemed to be impenetrable from the inside.

Logan sat up against a thick trunk of a pine tree. The rough bark scratched his back whenever he adjusted his position. Jenny sat next to him, cradling him with her arms, trying to keep him warm. Michael and Tristan had given him their coats. He wore Michael's because it was closer to his size. Tristan's coat lay over his legs, giving him some protection for his burns.

Logan had not looked at his legs yet. He did not know how serious the damage from the fire had been. Since coming inside the barrier, he had not tried to walk on his own. Would he have scars on his legs? Would he ever walk again? His pants were wet and cold, but it was refreshing on his burning skin. It helped subside the itching and searing of his thighs.

"How're you doing?" Jenny had not asked the question for a few minutes.

"A little better. Warming up a bit." Logan's shivering had calmed and his skin was beginning to return to its natural color.

"How're your legs?"

"They hurt, but not quite as badly as they did an hour ago."

"We've got to get you out of here and to a doctor," Jenny said.

Logan nodded. "Yeah, but the question is how?"

"Have you guys found anything yet?" she called to Michael and Tristan who were in the corner of the yard, close to the house.

118

"No," Michael called back. "If we could somehow get into the house, maybe we could find a way out from inside, but this stupid force field is right in front of the door. It won't let us through."

Tristan stood next to Michael, nodding in agreement.

Jenny turned back toward Logan. He could feel her warm breath on his cheek. It calmed him. "So, why do you think you could come into the yard, but we can't get out of it? You walked right through the barrier and it didn't even affect you."

Logan stared straight ahead, trying to summon all his strength. "I'm not sure. I just did it. I wasn't thinking straight at the time. All I know is that I didn't feel anything when I walked through it."

"But you knew we wouldn't be able to get out. You told us that right away."

"It's pretty clear someone or something is trying to keep us prisoner. It makes sense that there would be a trap. I escaped the front yard, so whoever is keeping us here probably knew I would come back to help you guys out. I'm guessing this thing let me in." Logan grimaced and put his hand on his right leg.

"Your burns?" Jenny asked.

"Yeah."

"Do you think you can get up to walk?"

"I'm not sure. Right now we don't have much reason to walk, do we?"

"We'll find a way out. You found a way out of the front yard."

Logan had told Jenny, Michael, and Tristan about the fire and the creek. About how he jumped through the flames and then found relief in the icy water.

"Yeah, and look at me now," Logan complained.

"You're gonna be fine. I think it's amazing what you did. I would have sat in that yard forever before I jumped through fire. How did you get the guts to do that?"

"There was really no choice. It was the only way out. I think you underestimate yourself. People do crazy things when their lives are at stake. You would've done the same."

"I don't know about that."

The two of them sat in silence for a moment, watching Michael and Tristan scour the perimeter of the yard, looking for any kind of clue that would help them escape.

"There may still be some hope," Logan said.

"What do you mean?"

"The reason we're out here in the first place."

"Zach?"

Logan nodded. "He knows something. He was right all along about this ghost-thing. Maybe he knows how to beat it."

"But how do you know he hasn't been captured too. How do you know he isn't in that house somewhere or out in the woods behind some kind of barrier like we are?"

"I don't know that. The part of the house I was in was empty, but I didn't even know about the addition until I was outside. I have no idea how to get into that part of the house. So, I guess Zach could be anywhere. But I do know that if anyone could survive a situation like this, it would be Zach. He can do pretty much anything when he really wants to."

Jenny nodded.

Logan continued. "But if he's still out there looking, I hope he finds us soon because something tells me we aren't going to be left alone too much longer. Whatever this thing is, it must have a plan and I don't think we want to know what it is."

Jenny's skin was pale and her eyes were wide. "Logan, what is this thing? That ghost in the woods that brought us here . . . what was that? These things aren't supposed to exist. I've never been so scared."

Logan took Jenny's hand and rested it on his leg, his hand on top of hers.

Michael and Tristan came running back to the tree.

"Did you find something?" Logan asked.

"Well, we have an idea," said Michael.

"Maybe we can go under it," said Tristan.

"Under it?" Logan was confused.

"Yeah," Michael began. "Over there on the side of the yard there's a tiny divot in the ground, so I reached my finger underneath and was able to pass it through to the other side with no shock or burn."

"We could dig a hole," Jenny said.

"Yeah, we could dig a hole under the barrier," Michael said.

"The only problem is how we do it," Tristan said. "We don't have a shovel and the ground is still too solid to do it with our hands."

"There is some kind of shed over there that might have some tools in it." Michael pointed toward a small, isolated structure with a rounded roof. "But it's on the outside of the barrier, so it won't do us much good."

Michael, Tristan, and Jenny looked at Logan. They seemed to be waiting for an answer, as if he knew how to solve every problem.

Logan thought for a moment. Then he spoke. "Look around on the ground. Try to find some rocks."

Jenny, Michael, and Tristan scoured the area. They each came back with a handful of medium sized stones.

"What are we gonna use these for?" asked Tristan.

"Do any of those have sharp edges?" Logan asked.

Michael understood. "This one might work," he said, holding up the pointed edge of one of his rocks.

"Okay, but we'll need more of those," Logan said.

"I'll go look for more," Tristan said. Tristan came back shortly with two other sharply pointed rocks.

Slowly, Logan grabbed the trunk of the pine tree he had been leaning against and pulled himself up.

Jenny held his arm for support.

As he bent his knees to stand, a sharp stinging pain flashed through his thighs. Logan grimaced, but he didn't let out a cry. He braced himself by putting his hand on the tree.

When Logan had reached a standing position, Jenny let go of his arm. Hoping not to topple over, Logan cautiously released his hand from the tree trunk. He was weak. He was wobbly. But he was standing on his own.

With a smile, Logan said, "Well, what are we waiting for? It's gonna take us a while to dig a whole with just a bunch of rocks." Logan then took his first delicate step toward the barrier.

Michael, Tristan, and Jenny followed closely behind, the rocks firmly in their hands.

Chapter 21

Zach

ZACH AND HIS DAD HAD been walking swiftly along the path. Robert led the way. He knew the exact point where they would need to break off the trail to find Victor's cabin.

Zach's eyes were beginning to burn with exhaustion. If he had had a mirror, he knew how his eyes would look—bloodshot and puffy, like the mornings after he and Logan's sleepovers. His stomach was an empty vacuum. The protein bar his dad gave him had helped, but he needed more. Despite all of this, he was still able to walk at a brisk pace, with renewed energy. He was like Perseus, his Andromeda waiting for him.

"Here, this is it," Robert said. "Look at this tree." Zach's dad pointed to the bark of a skinny birch tree. On the side of the trunk were two small letters written in black marker.

"CS." Zach paused for a moment, gathering his thoughts. He turned to his dad. "Chris Sutton?"

"Yeah. I marked it so I would know how to get back to the cabin, if it ever showed up again."

"Good thinking. So, where do we go from here?"

"I think if we walk directly south from this tree for about fifteen minutes or so, we should run into the cabin. Or, at least the clearing where the cabin should be."

"Dad, trust me. I'm positive the house will be there this time. I'm not sure how I know, but I just do," Zach said.

Zach's dad nodded.

ZACH AND HIS FATHER BEGAN their trek through the woods at an even quicker pace than before, with Zach leading the way, Chris's stone securely in his pocket. The stone seemed to be guiding him. He placed his hand on his pocket as he ran, making sure it was still there. He hadn't told his dad about the rock yet. It was only for him right now. His magic wallet. His winged sandals.

He moved magically through the thick brush with the fluency and ease of a galloping deer. He could sense he was close to Victor's home. To Michael and Tristan. To Chris. His dad grunted and gasped for air behind him.

Zach slowed down a bit. Looking straight ahead, he asked, "You okay, Dad?"

"I'm fine. We should be there soon," he said, trying to catch his wind.

Zach moved even quicker now. It was as if the woods had become his home. He seemed to know every branch, every twig, every ditch and divot in the ground. There were no scratches or welts on his hands or face this time. He eluded the dagger branches with an unconscious ease.

Zach stopped running. His father's footsteps crunched behind him.

Robert, with hands to his knees, panted trying to get air. "Why . . . did . . . you . . . stop?"

"Look. Around that big tree." Zach pointed into a clearing. No trees. No brush. It looked like someone's yard.

"That's it," Zach's dad said. "That's where the cabin was. But, just like I told you, it's just a clearing. No house."

Zach inched forward, peering around the remaining trees. His dad was right. There was no building at all, just an empty space where the trees had been cut down. He stood at the edge of the forest, the clearing directly in front of him. He toed the border between sanctuary and peril.

Robert stood a few steps behind Zach. "Zach, buddy. I think we should head back to the camp and let everyone know you're all right. Your mother and your teachers are worried sick about you. There's nothing to see. I'm sorry, but this is exactly what I ran into the last time I was here."

Zach didn't listen. Instead, he lifted his right foot out of the leaves and wet snow. Then he took one step forward into the clearing.

As he placed his wet shoe on the ground, the space in front of him transformed. The cabin they had been searching for appeared simultaneously with Zach's presence. The sun's rays reflected off the windows directly into his eyes.

It was as if the home knew he had come.

It had been *waiting* for him to come.

Mr. Sutton stood next to him now. His mouth wide open. His eyes round like quarters. "That's it. That's the house I saw the first time I came here. How did it just appear like that?"

"I don't know, Dad. None of this stuff makes any sense, does it?" Zach's dad shook his head.

"So, what do we do now?" Zach asked.

Robert was still shaking his head.

"Dad? What do we do?"

His dad looked at him. "We go in. We go in and find your friends. And we go find Chris," he said.

Zach nodded. The cabin didn't look scary. It didn't look like a witch had lived there. It was a log cabin. One you might see on a family vacation in the north woods or on a lake. Nothing out of the ordinary. But Zach's hands trembled. Drops of sweat dripped down from his forehead on to his cheek. And the emptiness in his gut was no longer a side effect of hunger.

Zach and his dad walked side by side toward the cabin. They moved at a slow pace, their eyes darting in every direction.

Then as suddenly as it had appeared, the cabin was gone.

"No!" cried Robert.

Zach stared straight ahead at the empty space. The trickling sound of a creek pulled his attention away. He gazed across the clearing. Behind where the home had stood was a rectangular, blue, metallic glow. Some kind of fence or barrier. It looked to outline what would have been the backyard of the cabin.

Zach edged closer. Were those people inside the barrier?

He turned around. "Dad! Look . . ."

His dad interrupted him. "Zach, I think I know why the cabin disappeared again."

"Why?"

"Because I came with you. I was allowed to see the cabin once, but only once. Victor is teasing me. The house appeared when you stepped out into the clearing, but once I started walking with you, it disappeared."

"Why would you being here make any difference?"

"Victor took Chris for a reason. You're his brother." Robert looked toward the absent home. Then he turned back to Zach and looked him straight in the eye. He put both hands on Zach's shoulders. "You said that Victor wants something from you. You aren't the youngest Sutton of this family, so I don't know why, but Zach, I'm beginning to think you're right. It's you he wants. It kills me to say this, but there is only one way to find your roommates and Chris. You go without me. You face Victor alone. If I stay back, I'm sure the home will reappear."

"What am I supposed to do when I get there? How do I fight a ghost witch? How can I possibly win that battle?"

Robert took a deep breath. "Zach, I'd be lying if I said I knew. But remember, you knew something about this place. You knew that house would be there. And I'm betting that you will know what to do when you get inside."

Zach put his head down. "Dad," he began. "When you showed up here, I got reenergized. I couldn't wait to continue this search. But now that we're here, I'm scared."

Zach's dad bent down to his level, his hand still on Zach's left shoulder. "Zach, if you don't feel good about this, let's go back. You don't have to go. There's no shame in that. Trust me, I understand."

Zach still stared at the ground.

His dad pulled him closer and hugged him tightly. His father's strong hands gripped his shoulder blades. "It's okay, buddy," he whispered. "Let's go back to camp. We can figure this out later. We'll figure out another way. I promise."

A quiet peace passed between the two, Zach still in his father's arms.

Finally, Zach looked up at his dad. "Dad, if we don't take care of this now, it will never end." He reached into his pocket and pulled out Chris's stone. "I don't know what's gonna happen when I go up there. Maybe the cabin will reappear, maybe it won't. But I do know my friends are in trouble." Zach pointed to the glowing barrier. "I know they're in there. And if there is any chance of finding Chris, I have to try."

"Zach, are you sure?"

"No. Not at all. But I have to do it anyway."

"Zach, listen to me. If you have any trouble, if you aren't sure what to do, just run. Do you hear me? Get out of there as fast as you can. I'll be waiting in the woods. Hopefully if I stay far enough away, that thing will let you in."

"Dad," Zach said with a smirk. "You know I can run."

Robert laughed half-heartedly. Then he looked at Zach's hand. "What is that?" he asked.

Zach opened his palm, revealing the rock. He held it out in front of him, so his father could see.

His dad placed his finger on the stone, rubbing it gently. "It looks like something Chris would have found."

Zach nodded. "Yeah, it is."

"You still have one of Chris's rocks?" Robert asked. "But I don't remember this one."

"He found it in Duluth that day. I took it from the hotel room."

A tear dropped from Mr. Sutton's eye.

"Dad, I don't think this is just another one of Chris's rocks. There's something different about this one. Something special. Victor may have special powers, but I think this rock does too."

"What kind of powers?" Robert asked.

Zach looked back to where the cabin had been. "I'm not exactly sure, Dad, but it's time I found out."

Chapter 22

ZACH MOVED OUT INTO the clearing. He tried to postpone the encounter by walking as slowly as he could. His dad had gone back into the forest, watching.

The figures inside the barrier had become more defined as Zach crept closer. There were three boys and a girl. If Michael and Tristan were there, who were the other two? Zach opened his mouth, ready to call Michael and Tristan's names, but before he could, the log cabin reappeared in front of him. His dad had been right. Victor—this witch, this ghost, wanted only him. The cabin beckoned him to enter.

The home blocked the view of the four people in back. He would have to go around the building to reach them.

Zach moved to his right and walked up the side of the front yard. The sound of the rushing creek followed him as he made his way closer to the house. When he reached the corner of the front porch, he reached his hand out to touch the wooden support beam that stretched from the railing to the roof. It was solid. Not a hologram. Not a figment of his imagination. A real, tangible structure.

He walked along the side of the home, his left hand sliding along the wall. A splinter in his finger made the home that much more real. He peered into the windows as he made his way around the house. An empty living area. A small, practical kitchen.

Attached to the back of the kitchen, the wood was fresher and cleaner. A large, open den with a piano. It seemed like a different home. An addition to the original structure. The addition Miranda had told him about.

Zach came to a dark room with a table in the middle. Were those rocks on the table? He pressed his nose against the window, trying to get a cleaner look. The shadows made it difficult to see, but there appeared to be a circle of rocks on the lone table. Miranda had said Victor built the addition to do some "pretty creepy stuff". Zach wondered what the circle of rocks was used for. Could they be related to Chris's stone in some way?

Zach reached the back corner of the cabin. He stopped and stood with his back against the wall, cowering, postponing the inevitable. He closed his eyes and took a deep breath, slowing his fluttering heart.

Peering around the corner, the bright, glowing barrier stood ten feet in front of him. It was partially translucent. The four figures on the inside were blurred a bit, but their identities became clear. They were standing on the far side of the backyard, by the opposite barrier wall. Tristan and Michael were bending down digging a hole in the dirt. Logan and Jenny sat next to them, watching intently.

"Hey!" Zach called.

The four of them jerked their heads in Zach's direction.

"Whatch y'all up to?" he said in his playful, southern twang.

Michael, Tristan, and Jenny sprinted to Zach's side of the yard. Logan limped slowly behind them.

Zach took a step closer to the barricade.

"Wait!" Jenny yelled. "Don't come any closer, Zach!"

Zach didn't take another step. He waited anxiously for his friends to reach him.

"You can't come in here," Michael said. "There is no way out. You can help us better on the outside."

Jenny and Tristan nodded.

Logan finally reached the others. He put his hand on Jenny's shoulder for support. "I had . . . a feeling . . . you'd find us," he huffed.

"Well, that's what I do, right? Bail you out?"

"I guess," laughed Logan.

"Wait a minute," Zach said. "I'm so confused. I knew Michael and Tristan were out here somewhere, but how did you two find your way into this mess?" he asked, pointing at Logan and Jenny.

"It's a long story," Jenny said.

"Yeah. We'll tell you all about it once we get out of here, but right now, we could use your help," Logan said.

Zach could see Logan was physically struggling. "You okay?" he asked.

"I'll live." Logan gave a reassuring smile. "Listen, we figure there is only one possible way out of this thing. We have to go underneath it."

"Is that what you guys are doing over there? Digging under the fence?"

"Yeah," said Michael. "But the rocks aren't exactly doing the trick. There's a shed on the other side, outside the barrier. There may be some tools in there or something. We can't get to it, but if you go around the house, you could. I think there's a lock on it, so we have to figure out how to get the door open."

Zach could see the shed through the barrier. "Okay. Let's get you guys out of there. I'll meet you on the other side."

Zach ran back alongside the cabin to the front yard. He stopped and stood facing the front steps. Something is in there. Waiting for me. He took one step toward the cabin. Then another. Then another, until he stood on the first stair leading up to the porch. Zach shook his head violently. "My friends are trapped back there. I've gotta get them out," he said partly to himself, and partly to whatever awaited him inside the cabin.

He jumped off the step and sprinted around the other side of the house, finding his way to the shed in the backyard. His friends waited for him, watching from inside their prison.

"Is this the shed?" Zach asked, looking at them over his shoulder.

"Yeah," Logan said. "That's it. You've got to get that padlock off somehow."

Zach studied the lock. The wood surrounding it was old and rotted. "I bet I can do it without actually breaking the lock."

"How?" Tristan asked.

"You'll see," Zach said.

He walked ten paces, turned around, and sprinted toward the structure. He took off and did a flying kick into the door of the shed.

The wood anchoring the lock cracked, loosening the door. Zach walked back to his starting point. He turned to the four prisoners. "I took karate when I was seven. I think I still got it."

Logan, Jenny, and Tristan could not help but laugh.

"I'm betting one more kick like that should do it," Zach said. Again, he broke into a sprint, soared through the air, and jabbed the door of the shed with his right foot. This time, the wood shattered, causing the door to cave into the shed. Zach landed smoothly on both feet.

"Nice work, Karate Kid," Logan said. "What do you see in there?"

Zach pushed the door open and scanned the shed for helpful tools. He turned to face his friends. "Jackpot," he said. He came out of the shed with two spades and two rakes. "This might help."

"Nice work," said Tristan.

Zach began digging on the outside of the barrier, while Michael, Tristan, and Jenny dug from the inside. Jenny had insisted that Logan rest.

While they dug, Logan told Zach the story of how he and Jenny had found Michael and Tristan. Their search in the middle of the night. Being captured by the ghost. The fire, the creek, the burns on his legs.

Zach simply nodded, unfazed by the illogical story. In his new reality, logic no longer applied.

They continued to dig, making a small dent in the frozen soil.

"This is going to take forever to dig a hole big enough for us to fit through," Michael said.

"Yeah, but what other choice do we have?" Jenny said.

"Jenny's right. We have to try," said Zach. He continued to scrape at the ground as hard as he could. "Ahh!" Zach dropped the spade from his hands.

"What's wrong?" said Logan.

"The spade. The handle burnt my hands." Zach kicked the spade with his foot. "Did yours get hot?"

Michael, Tristan, and Jenny shook their heads.

Zach stuck his nose in the air. "Wait a minute," he said. "Do you guys smell that?" The foul odor had returned. Stronger than ever.

"I don't smell anything," Tristan said.

"No, me neither," said Jenny.

Michael shook his head.

Logan stared at Zach.

"Do you smell it, Logan?" asked Zach.

"I think you know that I don't."

Zach turned toward the cabin. He stared it down like a hunter eyeing its prey. Zach could feel his three friends looking on with curiosity. "Guys," he said, not taking his eyes off the cabin. "I have to go in there. Whatever it is that brought us here, it isn't going to let me help you in this way. You guys keep digging. When you get the hole big enough, get out of here and run as fast as you can back to camp. Do not wait for me. You understand?"

"We can't just leave you here," Jenny said.

"Yeah. We'll help you," said Tristan.

"No guys," Logan interrupted. "Zach's right. He has to deal with this. He'll meet us back at the camp. He'll be fine. Right, Zach?"

Zach nodded to Logan. Then he turned toward the cabin. "I gotta go. Remember, keep digging and get out of here as fast as you can," he said, looking back to his friends. Zach ran toward the front of the house, but stopped suddenly. He turned around to face the group of four one last time. "By the way, if you get out and need some help, my dad is in the woods over there on the north side of the cabin. He's waiting for us."

"Your dad's here?" said Logan, shocked. "How did he get here? Why isn't he with you?"

"It's a long story. When we all get out of here, I'll tell you all about it. I promise," Zach said.

Logan nodded. "I bet you will," he said.

Zach smiled, turned around, and ran as fast as he could toward the front door of the home. When he rounded the corner of the cabin, safely out of his friends' view, he slowed to a walk. Zach's expression turned stolid. He had the look of a rookie fire fighter staring into the bowels of a torrent of flames.

The inferno waited.

Zach hoped he would have the courage to face it.

Chapter 23

ZACH STOOD ON THE FRONT porch of the cabin, gripping the handle of the front door. He turned the handle and pushed his way into what looked to be the living room. He had seen the room briefly as he walked along the side of the house, but things had changed. This was not the empty, barren room he had seen earlier. It was furnished completely. A rust colored sofa and loveseat squared the center of the room. A rectangular coffee table sat in front of the sofa. Family photographs and paintings draped the four walls. This was a functional, living home. Victor had rolled out the red carpet for Zach.

He paced in and out of the furniture, searching for any clue that might help him understand what Victor was after.

A painting of a man and, presumably, his two sons hung on one of the walls. "Victor, Kristian and Mikko," said Zach. Underneath the picture was a small wooden table, which held a lamp and a bowl of rocks. Zach laid his hand on top of the stones, feeling the smooth and jagged edges of the various nuggets. "Chris," he whispered. "Are you here?" He spoke quietly to himself.

Light penetrated the cracks of a swinging door. An entrance to the next room. *Chris has to be here somewhere,* Zach thought. He moved swiftly to the door, but just as he had reached his hand out to push it open, a roar came from outside the cabin. The revving of an engine. Zach moved away from the door and to the window on the far side of the living room. The chugging sound of the engine was louder now, but there was no car.

Zach's palms were clammy, while his heart beat steadily faster. His dad had told him to run if he was in trouble. He wanted to run as fast as he could out of the house, back to the safety of his dad. But he didn't.

He stood in front of the window and waited, listening to the roar of the engine, wondering what Victor had in mind for him.

It appeared out of nowhere, like an airplane emerging from a cloud. The truck Zach had seen in the woods two days ago was now in front of Victor's home. But this wasn't the same beat-up, rusty, dead truck that lay in the forest that day. This truck looked brand new.

Zach squinted his eyes, bent down, and moved his head closer to the windowpane, trying to see inside the truck. Who was in the driver's seat?

The engine stopped. The silence was eternal. Zach looked at the front door. He could run out right now and forget all of this.

The driver's side door opened and from the truck emerged a man. He stood tall and had short, blond hair. His eyes were close together, making his rounded nose the focal point of his face. His mouth was wide, his lips full. He wore a flannel shirt, jeans, and heavy boots.

The man stood next to the door of the truck. He stared directly at Zach through the window. Zach stood tall and ducked out of the way of the window. Plastered against the wall, the painting of the man with his sons came into focus. Zach raised his eyebrows and tiptoed closer to the picture. One of the younger men sat on a chair below his father. He had short, blond hair.

Zach went back to the window. The man stood still with a stoic, somber look. "Kristian Leppla," Zach said. "Victor's dead son."

At any moment Kristian would be here, seeking his revenge much like his father had. Zach knew the house had a large addition on the back. He could sneak through the kitchen and find his way through the home. Maybe he could find a hiding place. Maybe Logan and the others had finished the hole and they could all escape together.

As Zach was about to dash through the swinging door, he stopped. This encounter with the Lepplas was inevitable. There was no point in postponing it.

Footsteps crept to the front door, the old, wooden porch creaking with every step. Zach turned to face the doorway, awaiting his inescapable fate.

The door opened. A man eased into the living room. His hair was sandy blond and he had large dimples on each cheek. His face was ghostly pale and wrinkled. He wore a thick denim, button down shirt and sturdy corduroy pants.

"Zach Sutton," he said.

Zach looked closely into the eyes of the man. This was not the same man he saw through the window. This was not Kristian Leppla. He glanced once again at the portrait on the wall. The dark eyes. The unmistakable dimples. Zach's stomach clenched.

Zach nodded. He did not make eye contact again with the man. Instead, he looked out the far window, grasping the stone in his pocket. His left hand fidgeted, wiping his brow, then dropped to his side. He closed his eyes briefly, gathering strength. He could feel the penetrating stare of the man standing in the doorway. Finally, Zach spoke. "Victor."

Victor moved slowly into the middle of the room. "You were expecting Kristian. Am I right?"

Zach backed away as Victor advanced.

"You haven't seen the last of Kristian, I promise."

Zach pressed against the wall nearest the creek. He could not back away any farther. "Why me?" he asked. "What do you want with me?"

"What do I want with you?" Victor chuckled. "What do I want with you? My son perished in flames and you dare to ask me what I want with you?"

"I had nothing to do with your son's death. I wasn't even alive!"

Victor sat down on the edge of the loveseat. "You're right, Zach. A lot of Sutinens . . . excuse me, Suttons . . . have paid for your great-great grandfather's evil. But, I lost my son and I promised Fredrik that every generation of his family would pay for his sins. I always keep my promises.

"Just picture it, Zach. My boy, only twenty-three years old, is driving to the logging plant to get a head start on his work for the day. A hard-working, motivated young man. There he is, sitting in the office doing some paperwork when all of a sudden, fire surrounds the building. Piles of logs rise up in flames. There was nowhere for him to go.

He had no chance. It had to have been started by someone. Burnt gas cans were left in the yard. Even the old truck was torched."

Zach listened to Victor's story. Gasoline. Flaming truck. Gasoline and burnt rubber. That odor had harassed Zach throughout the trip to Pine Ridge.

"Fredrik denied everything," Victor continued. He claimed he had nothing to do with it. He claimed it was an accident. But it was no accident that I had to bury my son. Fredrik didn't understand who he was dealing with. Unfortunately, you and your whole family have to pay for that."

"But I don't understand. The trend has always been that the youngest Sutton kids in a generation are cursed. My brother, Chris, is missing. I know you had something to do with that. So, what do you want with me?"

Victor got up easily from the sofa. He glided over to the small table. His shoes made no noise as they slid along the floor, like a snake.

Turning his back to Zach, he playfully fingered the bowl of rocks. "Your brother is just fine. I promise you that."

Zach's eyebrows rose to his hairline and his eyes widened. "Chris is alive? Where is he? Is he in this house?" Zach ran to the kitchen door.

"Yes, he is alive. But no, he is not in this house." Victor faced Zach now.

"So, where is he?"

Victor took one step closer to Zach. "I'd rather not talk about that right now. You asked me a question a minute ago. 'What did I want with you?'"

Zach took a step back. "Yeah. You have Chris. You're breaking the rules by coming after me too."

Victor chuckled. "Breaking the rules?" he said with a smile. "I created the rules. I can change them whenever I want." Victor walked around the sofa and stood a few paces in front of Zach. "But if it makes you feel any better, I didn't change the rules arbitrarily."

"Okay, so why did you change them?" Zach turned his head to see that there were only a few feet between him and the wall.

"I changed them because you have something I need."

"What could I possibly have that you need?"

"Zach, you're a smart kid. Think about it."

"I have no idea what you're talking about," said Zach.

Victor raised his eyebrows and smirked. His dimples accentuated the lines on his face. He waited silently for Zach to understand.

Zach leaned against the wall next to the window. He put his left hand in his pocket and pulled out Chris's stone. It was the only meaningful thing he possessed. The only thing Victor could possibly want. "Do you mean this?" he asked, lifting the rock in his palm.

"Now you're starting to use that head of yours," Victor said.

"But what does this have to do with—" Zach stopped in midsentence. He looked at the rock in his hand. "How did you know about this?"

"None of that matters, Zach. The important thing is that you give it to me now." Victor held out his hand.

Zach opened his palm and held the rock out in front of him. But as Victor reached for it, he snatched his hand back and fisted the stone.

Victor cocked his head to the right, his face emotionless. "Give me the rock, Zach."

"I want to know where Chris is," Zach said, holding the rock behind his back.

Victor stepped away and turned his back to Zach once again. He paced toward the other side of the room.

The window was directly to Zach's left. It was closed, but it was unlocked and it had no screen or storm window on the outside.

Victor turned to face Zach. "You want to know where Chris is?"

Zach's hand was on the windowpane. "Yeah. He's my brother and you took him. What did you do with him? If you really want this rock, you'll tell me."

"Do you really believe that you can call the shots, Zach?" Victor had moved closer to Zach now. He spoke just inches from his face, but with no breath, no element of life. "I control you. Those friends of yours imprisoned out back? I have no use for them. But I took them so I could reel you in, Zach. I knew you wouldn't hesitate to try to save them. You see, I don't think you understand the extent of my power. And as far as your brother is concerned, I'll tell you this much. If you don't hand over the stone, you will never find Chris."

Zach thought about the power of the rock. How it had warmed him when he needed it most. What could Victor do with this if he had it? Would he ever tell me where Chris was anyway? He doubted it.

"I have other ways of getting the rock from you if you don't hand it to me. Trust me," Victor said.

Zach still held the rock behind his back. Over Victor's left shoulder, through the far window, Zach saw a face. Logan. Jenny, Michael, and Tristan fell in behind him. All four of them peered through the window. Zach leaned to his left so Victor didn't block their view of him.

Victor turned quickly, wondering what Zach was looking at. As he saw Zach's friends, he rushed to the other side of the living room. But when he reached the window, they were gone.

Zach saw an opportunity. He shoved the rock back into his pocket. Then he grabbed the bottom of the window, threw it upward, pushed himself out with his forearms, and tumbled to the cold, snowy ground.

Zach jumped to his feet and sprinted around to the front of the house. Logan, Jenny, Michael, and Tristan waited for him in the front yard. Their clothes were covered in dirt. "You made it!" Jenny said.

"Who was that guy inside the house?" Tristan asked.

"Was it Victor?" Logan asked.

"Who's Victor?" said Tristan.

Zach caught his breath. "I don't have time to explain right now. We gotta go! Come on." He ran again, leading the other four toward the forest.

"Zach!" The deep, bellowing voice was unmistakable. "Where are you going, Zach?"

Zach stopped running. The others followed suit. Behind them, on the cabin's porch, Victor stood. His hands were on his hips.

"We aren't finished with our conversation yet," Victor said. He walked down the steps into the clearing. The home behind him became transparent. It gradually dissolved into the brisk air, leaving nothing but an empty lot. But Victor stayed. He walked toward Zach and his friends, the speed of his gait steadily increasing with every step.

"We gotta split up," Zach said. "He wants me, not you. You guys go that way, through the woods. It will lead you straight to Pine Ridge. I'll lead him this way." Zach pointed to opposite ends of the forest.

"We aren't gonna leave you alone," Logan said.

The others nodded in agreement.

"Don't worry about it. Trust me, I'll be fine," Zach said. "I'll meet you back at the camp."

Victor was getting closer. Suddenly, his arms transformed. They grew into long, dark tentacles, stretching outward like a pair of wings. Victor's face changed too. His pale features turned ghostly. His eyes became thin and bright, while his nose, mouth and dimples became dark, like the night sky. Victor's legs disappeared into his body, leaving only a black, floating spirit.

"Oh, God. That's the thing that captured me and Logan," said Jenny, panicking.

Victor's arms stretched out to Zach. "Run!" he yelled.

Logan, Jenny, Michael, and Tristan took off toward the woods.

Zach ran in the opposite direction, Victor's ghastly spirit flying close behind him.

"Come on, Zach. Run!" His dad's voice. He had emerged from the woods and he was beckoning him into the forest. When Zach hit the tree line, his dad grabbed him. "Hold on, Zach. That thing is gone."

Zach turned around. Victor's ghost had disappeared. "He's not gone," said Zach. "He's here somewhere. Dad, you shouldn't stay with me. Victor wants this rock I have." Zach showed his dad the stone. "I don't know why, but he's pretty serious about it."

"So, just give him the rock, son."

Zach shook his head. "I can't explain it, Dad, but I think if I give him this stone, it won't end there. It'll just get worse."

A dark shadow passed overhead. Zach and his father nervously scanned the forest. Through the trees, two bright, thin eyes stared at them.

"Dad, go that way." He pointed through the trees. "I can run faster on my own. I'll be fine. I'll figure something out."

Zach was gone before his dad could protest.

He weaved in and out of the tree branches, hurdling ditches and fallen trunks. He sensed the shadowy ghost of Victor following him.

Zach didn't stop. Not even when he reached the trail. His sprint quickened when he took a sharp left on to the cleared path.

Zach glanced over his shoulder. No Victor. But still, he didn't slow down.

The hill was straight ahead. The hill he had been climbing when his father found him. The camp wasn't far.

His breathing was heavy. His legs ached, climbing the steep incline. As the terrain flattened, the pain in Zach's thighs eased. He quickened his pace again. The trail curved sharply in and out of the forest.

The end of the trail. It was a few yards ahead of Zach. The roofs of buildings were partly shaded by tree branches. He had made it. Pine Ridge.

Zach looked over his shoulder again. No Victor. He looked to his left and to his right. Nothing but trees. He started forward again toward the camp, but just before he reached the fire pit he stopped. A dark shadow floated a few paces in front of him. Victor, with his bright, yellow eyes. His ghastly arms reached out for Zach. Before he could be swallowed by the specter, Zach turned to his right and sprinted back into the woods.

He curled through the trees, trying to find an entrance to Pine Ridge. Zach emerged from the trees in front of a giant structure. It towered above him like a skyscraper.

Victor was nowhere to be found.

He recognized where he was. He had been here just yesterday.

The ropes course.

Zach had hoped to find his classmates or teachers when he returned. He hoped Victor would stay away if there were others around. But there was no one in sight. No teachers. No friends.

He stood at the rear of the course. The entrance to the first obstacle was fifty yards in front of him. *Maybe I can make it out of here and back to the dorms before Victor finds me*, he thought.

He sprinted toward the entrance of the ropes course, but before he got there, he slowed to a walk. Then he stopped. If I escape now, then what? Victor would track me down. This would never end.

Zach felt the stone in his pocket. He remembered Perseus. The hero's journey. Killing Medusa. Defeating the Kraken.

He had to face Victor now.

Instead of exiting the ropes course, he climbed to the first obstacle. He had no harness. No protection if he should lose his balance. He steadied his way across the single cord, holding on to the two rope railings. He worked slowly and carefully.

When he reached the platform, he pulled himself up, relieved to feel the solid floor below him. He breathed in. Then out. He scanned the area, looking for Victor.

Quiet. Only the sound of a few chirping birds who had returned from their winter sojourn. Victor was nowhere to be found.

The next obstacle. A wooden bridge, which led to the highest platform on the ropes course. Zach ran up the bridge, feeling the vibration of the shaking wood below him.

He reached the summit of the ropes course. A bead of sweat dripped from his forehead. Zach stood tall, eye level with the top of the forest. The cafeteria and dorms loomed in the distance. He wouldn't miss anything from up here. He would see Victor coming from a mile away.

He stood on the platform, waiting. He held the railing with his left hand, while gripping the pocketed stone with his right. Zach's head was on a swivel, turning from left to right, anticipating Victor's arrival.

A half hour had passed. Zach's ankles and thighs began to ache. Needing to rest, he sat on the platform, his legs dangling over the edge. Why is he not coming? What's Victor waiting for?

In the distance, kids' voices echoed through the woods. Zach pulled himself to his feet. Through the trees a pack of students made their way toward the ropes course. They would be here soon. Victor would never show his face then.

Zach scanned the forest one last time, looking for the ghost. Finding nothing, he took his hand from his pocket and stepped on to the bridge, anxious to return to camp.

"Hello, Zach." A familiar voice.

Zach stopped, one foot on the platform and one foot on the bridge. He pulled his foot from the wooden crossing, planted both feet on the platform, and turned toward the voice.

Victor stood on the third obstacle's landing. He was no longer the dark, shadowed figure. This was Victor as Zach had seen him in the cabin. Blond hair. Pale. Dimples. Weathered face.

"You shouldn't have run, Zach. You're just making it harder on yourself."

"I'm not running anymore," Zach said.

"That's true. I'm glad you've come to your senses. Why don't you just give me what I want and we can end this now."

In the distance, the students' voices were becoming louder.

Zach pulled the stone from his pocket. "If I give you this now, nothing will end. This curse you've put on my family won't stop and it will probably only get worse. You can't fool me. This rock is powerful. I know that now." Zach looked down at the stone in his palm. "It may even help me find Chris," he whispered to himself. He looked back at Victor. "If you want this, you're gonna have to take it from me."

Zach clenched the muscles in his arms and legs, bracing for whatever Victor had in store for him.

Victor nodded, a half smile on his face. "I see," he said.

Zach could sense the evil in Victor's eyes.

Victor stretched his arms out at his sides, darkness taking over, morphing his limbs into shadows. His ghostly arms stretched out above the ropes course obstacles, searching for Zach.

Zach trembled at the sight of Victor's human face and body combined with the arms of a dark spirit.

His muscles stiff, Zach clasped the stone tightly in his hand. Victor's arms moved slowly toward him. He turned toward the bridge and looked down over the side of the platform, searching for a quick escape. He couldn't jump from here and with no harness he would have to travel back through the course slowly. Victor would surely capture him and the rock.

Zach was trapped. There was nowhere to go.

Victor's arms were closer now, the dark fingers reaching for him.

There was only one option. Zach released the tension in his body, stood tall, and cupped the stone in both of his hands.

He brought the rock to his forehead and closed his eyes. Breathe in. Breathe out. Slowly. Calmly.

Even with eyes closed, he could sense Victor's arms almost upon him.

Zach opened his eyes, the ghostly hands a few feet in front of his face.

He was on a pitcher's mound now, staring down Victor like an opposing batter. This was Zach's turf. His element.

The windup.

With all his strength, all his courage, Zach hurled Chris's stone at Victor just as the ghost's arms tapped his cheeks.

The rock tore through the air like a meteor. When it reached Victor, it penetrated the middle of his chest, where his heart would have been. The black arms catapulted backward, separating from Victor's body. They dissipated into the pure air of the forest.

Victor stood, squinting his eyes at Zach. There was no defeat in him.

A bright light appeared where the rock had pierced his chest, blinding Zach momentarily. Then the ghost's figure shattered into millions of fragments, like stars dissolving into the atmosphere.

Chris's stone dropped from the ghost's body and fell to the ground.

Zach stared into the once evil space. Victor was gone.

Chapter 24

THE STUDENTS' VOICES WERE closer now, almost at the ropes course.

Zach climbed on to the two wire supports and held tightly to the rope railings above, shuffling his way across to the next obstacle. He made his way across the two parallel logs with ease, finding himself at the zip line.

With no harness, Zach could not attach himself to the line. He studied the mechanism, then looked back to the rest of the course. He could go back the way he came. He examined the zip line again. He would have to hang on to the karabiners with his hands.

The kids were closer now.

Zach grabbed the karabiners on the zip line, took a deep breath and leaped from the platform. His eyes watered and the metal of the karabiners scraped his hands. Gravity punished Zach's stretched arms.

Reaching the ground safely, he dropped his hands, letting them fall loosely to his sides.

The pack of students walked down the trail toward the course. Zach didn't recognize any of them. From another school, probably.

He turned back toward the course and ran as fast as he could to the obstacle where the rock had fallen. He crouched to his knees and scoured the ground, looking for the stone. Its white color would make it hard to find in the snow. He slid his hands along the cold slush. Pebbles. Pine needles. And then . . . a rock. It sat on top of the snow like a trophy, waiting to be retrieved. Zach grabbed it and it instantly warmed his palm.

Zach stood tall and jammed the stone back into his pocket. The group of students trickled into the grounds of the ropes course.

Zach walked past the group, finding his way back to the trail. He kept his eyes straight ahead, feeling the stares of the students upon him.

"Can I help you?" It was the voice of a Pine Ridge employee. She wore the mandatory green vest.

Already part way up the hill, Zach turned to face the woman who had called to him. "No, thanks. I'm okay. I gotta get back to my group."

The woman jogged up the hill to speak to him. She had short, brown hair with long, skinny legs. Her nametag said Jocelyn. "What's your name?" she asked.

"Zach."

"Zach Sutton?"

"Yeah."

"Thank goodness. There are a lot of people looking for you. Let me walk you back to your group."

They hiked side by side, Jocelyn asking all sorts of questions. "Where did you go? Did you get cold? Hungry?"

Zach put his head down and walked silently.

"Zach, we're going to need to know if you're okay. Are you all right?"

Zach froze. His hands had been in his pockets while Jocelyn had bombarded him with questions. The stone never left his palm.

He gazed off into the shadows of the woods. Still staring at the trees, he said, "I'm all right. For now, at least."

Chapter 25

W HEN ZACH AND JOCELYN REACHED the campfire pit, the campus was quiet. His friends and classmates were nowhere to be found.

"Where is everyone?" he asked.

"I think most of them are over there in the parking lot." Jocelyn pointed to the yellow school bus parked on the other side of the cafeteria.

"Is everyone leaving? What's going on?"

"I'm not sure what the plan is exactly. But I know everyone had a pretty good scare when you and the others disappeared, so I wouldn't be surprised if you're all heading home. Why don't we head over to the bus and see what's going on. I think they'll be pretty happy to see you." Jocelyn smiled, leading Zach toward the parking lot.

Zach followed behind her. On the left side of the school bus, three police cars were parked side by side. They were empty. On the right side of the bus were five other cars. One was a tan Honda Accord. Exactly like his . . .

"Zach!"

Mom's voice.

She ran down the path from the administration building and grabbed Zach, pulling him close to her. "You're here. I'm so glad you're here. I thought I'd lost you too." She clenched him like a vice, swaying back and forth, her frizzy hair rubbing against his cheek.

"I'd better get back to my students down at the ropes course," Jocelyn said. "I'm glad you're okay, Zach." Jocelyn gave a wave and left Zach and his mom alone.

"Thanks," said Zach. "Mom, you're kind of crushing me here."

She loosened her grip. "Are you okay? Where have you been? You scared me to death, Zach. The whole drive up here I wondered if I would ever see you again."

"I'm fine, Mom. Have you seen Dad?"

"No, but I just got here a few minutes ago. Honey, you don't look fine. You're all scratched up. What happened?"

Zach didn't answer right away. "I . . . I just went out to do some exploring and got lost."

Zach's mother hugged him again. "What is going on with you, honey? Why do you keep pulling these crazy stunts?"

The door of the administration building opened. Jenny, Michael, and Tristan wandered out on to the path.

"Mom . . . Umm . . . I'll be right back, okay?" Zach backed away from his mother and walked quickly up the path to meet his friends. "You made it," he said.

"Yeah, we're okay," Jenny said. "You pointed us in the right direction. We just had to battle the forest and some hills, but it didn't take long to get back here."

"How'd you get away from that thing?" Tristan asked.

"I wouldn't exactly say I got away from him."

"So, what happened?" Michael asked.

Zach looked into the eyes of his allies. He then turned around to see his mom, watching him, her arms wrapped around her body. "Where's Logan?" he asked, changing the subject.

"He's inside. They have a medical clinic in the back. A nurse is checking him out."

"Is he gonna be okay? Can I go see him?"

Jenny answered, "I think he's going to be fine, but we haven't seen him since he got in there. Maybe you can go in?" She looked at Michael and Tristan for confirmation. They nodded. "The nurse will probably want to take a look at you too," Tristan said. "You look pretty beat up."

"I'm fine. Just some scrapes and bruises. Nothin' big."

They were interrupted when the door to the admin building opened. Logan emerged, hobbling on crutches. "Hey, you made it!" He rocked himself over to Zach, and then held out his right hand.

Zach gave him a high-five. "Yeah, I'm here. But what about you? You look terrible."

"My right thigh stings a little, but the nurse says they're pretty minor burns. They were worried I had hypothermia from being in that creek, but I checked out okay. I'm supposed to go to the doctor as soon as I can. My mom's in there talking to the nurse right now."

"Your mom is up here?"

"Yeah. All of our parents are here," Logan said. "When we disappeared, Lomeier called them and they all came."

Zach turned back to his mom. He waved to her.

She waved back.

"Have you guys seen my dad? Did he make it back?" he asked, facing Logan and the others again.

They were silent. Everyone looked away from Zach, except Logan. "We haven't seen him," he said.

"He'll probably show up," Jenny added.

"He should have been back by now," Zach said, looking around frantically. Zach looked back at Logan. *Miranda*, he thought. Maybe she knows something. Maybe Dad went to see her. "I have to go."

"Zach, where are you going? You just got back!" Logan called as Zach ran down the path toward the cafeteria.

"Zach? What's going on?" his mom asked as he sprinted past her.

"I'll be right back!" Zach called.

Zach barged into the cafeteria and made his way to the kitchen. "Dad? Miranda? Are you here?" He looked around the cafeteria, but it was empty. The only sound was a faucet running in the back of the kitchen. "Miranda? Are you back there?" he called just as the cafeteria door opened behind him. Zach turned around.

"Zach!" his dad called, hugging his son.

Zach wrapped his arms around his father. "Where were you?"

"I just got here. I tried to follow you in the woods, but I'm not in the shape I used to be," he said with a smile. "I had to find my way back to the trail. It took some time. I saw your mother outside and she told me you ran in here. What are you looking for?"

"I was looking for you. I thought you might have come here to—" Before he could finish, Zach heard footsteps emerging from the kitchen.

"Hello, Zach."

Zach backed away from his father, turning toward the familiar voice. "Dad, this is Miranda."

Robert's smile vanished.

"Nice to meet you," she said, holding out her hand.

Robert looked at Zach and then at Miranda. "Miranda Leppla?"

"That's right," she said.

"My son has told me a lot about you," he said, shaking hands with Victor's granddaughter.

"Has he?" Miranda rubbed Zach's head. "So, Zach, you decided to go on a little adventure, I hear."

Zach looked up at her. "I guess you could call it that," he said.

Miranda looked back at Zach's dad. "You have a very brave boy here."

Robert nodded. "Yes, I do," he said, looking at Zach. "Miranda, I understand you've given Zach some help."

"I don't know about that, but let's just say, Zach and me have some things in common," Miranda said.

Robert nodded.

"Zach, I'm sorry for ignoring you during KP duty," Miranda said. "You were looking for answers and I abandoned you. I'm afraid to talk about my grandfather in front of others."

"It's okay," he said. "I get it."

Miranda looked Zach in the eye. "You know where to find me," she said.

"Find you for what?" Zach asked.

Robert pulled his son closer to him. Zach could feel his dad's strong hand on his shoulder.

Miranda smiled. "Even heroes need help sometimes," she said.

"So, WHAT DID YOU TELL everyone when you got back?" Zach asked his friends as they huddled in the parking lot. Zach's dad was talking to his mom outside the cafeteria. "Did you tell them about Victor and the house?"

Logan, Jenny, Michael, and Tristan shot glances at each other, smiling. Then Logan explained. "As soon as we found our way out of the woods we made a pact. None of us were gonna say anything about Victor Leppla or the disappearing cabin."

"No one would have believed us anyway," said Michael.

No one but Miranda, Zach thought. "You're probably right," he said, nodding. "So, what *did* you tell them?"

"The police had been searching for us. When we got back a couple of cops were with Lomeier, so we talked to them first," Logan said. "We kept it simple," he said with a grin.

Michael interrupted. "Tristan and I told the police and Mrs. Lomeier that we had wandered off into the woods because we had heard a wolf cry. I've always wanted to see a wolf, so I had to go, right?" he said. "We never found the wolf, but we did manage to get ourselves lost. Luckily for us, Logan and Jenny found us and led us back to camp."

"All the credit goes to you, Zach," said Jenny.

"What do you mean?"

"You went searching for Michael and Tristan first. We never would have found them had we not come after you," she explained. "You're a hero," she said, playfully slugging Zach in the arm.

Zach nodded. Then he looked at Michael and Tristan. "Your wolf story has some truth to it, you know."

"What do you mean?" Tristan asked.

"The wolf found you," Zach said.

Everyone nodded quietly.

Jenny broke the silence. "You never explained how you got away. What happened after we separated?"

Zach looked away from his friends.

"Zach?" Logan said. "What happened?"

"Let's just say that Victor's gone."

"What do you mean, 'he's gone?'" asked Michael.

"He's gone. For now anyway."

Zach's friends looked confused, but didn't pry any further.

"Hey, look behind you," Logan said, pointing.

Zach turned around. His mom and dad were hugging. Something Zach had not seen them do for a long time. Not since the day Chris went missing.

"Zach, I think the police might want to talk to you," Logan said, pointing up the walkway. Two police officers were walking toward them, Mrs. Lomeier following behind.

Zach ignored Logan. Instead, he jogged over to his mom and dad. He stood next to them as they embraced. His mom and dad put their arms around Zach, pulling him closer.

Not even a magical stone could warm him like this.

Chapter 26

BEFORE ZACH LEFT WITH HIS MOM, Adam and Mitch jumped off the bus. They high-fived him. "Glad you made it back!" Adam shouted.

"Yeah, everyone was freakin' out," Mitch added.

Mr. Foster put his arm around him and asked, "You okay?"

Mr. Pliska and all the other teachers also said their goodbyes. Even Mrs. Lomeier gave him a hug. "I'm glad you're safe," she said, squeezing him tightly.

And just before Zach got into the car, Miranda came out of the cafeteria. He saw her through the trees. She stood right outside the door, holding up her hand. A wave.

Zach waved back, wondering if he would see her again.

ZACH SAT IN THE FRONT SEAT of his mom's Honda Accord. He stared out the window watching the trees go by. They had been driving for twenty minutes in silence. Unusual for his mom.

He finally broke the silence. "What were you and Dad talking about back there?"

His mom stared straight ahead, not concentrating on the road, but on something else.

"Mom?"

"Yeah, honey?"

"I asked you what you and Dad were talking about back at Pine Ridge, before you hugged him."

"Oh, uh . . . we were just really happy you were safe. We were both so worried."

"That's all?"

She paused. "Well, he did say something else."

"What was it?" Zach wondered how much she knew about Victor Leppla, if anything.

"He told me he found you in the woods."

"Yeah, he did."

His mom nodded. "But then he said you two were separated."

"We were."

"I asked your father how that happened."

"Wh . . . What did he say?" asked Zach.

"All he said was that he would explain some other time." Zach's mom looked puzzled. "But then he did say one other thing."

"What was it?"

"Chris. He said he thinks there's still a chance to find Chris. But he wouldn't tell me anymore than that."

Zach faced straight ahead, staring at the painted yellow lines on the highway as they marked the car's progress.

"Do you know anything about this, Zach? What happened out there? What happened in those woods? Do you know something about Chris's disappearance?"

Zach was silent for a moment, not knowing what to say. Why didn't his dad tell her the truth? Why has he kept this from her for so long? Finally, he spoke. "Mom, if I tell you something, will you promise to believe me?"

"Of course I'll believe you, honey. What is it? You can tell me. Do you know something about Chris?"

Zach breathed deeply through his nose. Then he began. "A long time ago there was this guy named Victor Leppla . . ."

Epilogue

THE FOREST WAS DARK. Stars enveloped the night sky, the full moon shone brightly. Students slept in the dormitories. Birds and squirrels rummaged through leaves and pine needles.

Underneath the ropes course lay thousands of tiny fragments. The pieces were too small to be seen by the human eye. The kids on the course had had no idea what lay below them. They had no clue that evil waited at their feet.

The fragments rose from the snowy ground, emitting a pale, blue light. Up they went, higher and higher, floating like tiny butterflies, and finally merging on the logs of the ropes course.

They came together piece by piece, the glow becoming brighter with each connection. They formed a shape. The shape of a man. He was tall and pale, with dimples on either side of his mouth.

When all the pieces joined, the man balanced steadily on the logs, his arms at his sides. And then . . . he smiled.